Eye of the Father

EYE
of the
FATHER

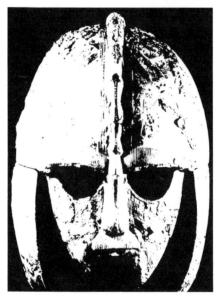

David Williams

ANANSI
Toronto   Buffalo   London   Sydney

Cover design: Laurel Angeloff
Author photograph: David Carey

The author is grateful to the Canada Council and to the University of Manitoba for monies granted during the writing of this novel. The Department of External Affairs, the SSHRCC, and CP Air also helped greatly, the one by organizing a reading tour of Scandinavia, the other two by underwriting travel to a conference at the University of Aarhus, Denmark. Finally, Sverre Sornes bestowed Hardangerfjorden, both then and now, from the helm of his boat one spring.

Published with the assistance of the Canada Council and the Ontario Arts Council, and printed in Canada for
House of Anansi Press Limited
35 Britain Street
Toronto, Ontario M5A 1R7

Canadian Cataloguing in Publication Data

Williams, David, 1945-
    Eye of the father

(Anansi fiction series; AF 49)
ISBN 0-88784-144-9.

I. Title. II. Series.

PS8595.I4762E93 1985/   C813'.54   C85-098405-X
PR9199.3.W543E93 1985

50,970   1   2   3   4   5   /   90   89   88   87   86   85

for Granny
and for Jeremy and Bryan

Alone I sat   when the Old One sought me
The terror of gods,   and gazed in mine eyes:
"What hast thou to ask?   why comest thou hither?
Othin, I know   where thine eye is hidden."

The Wise-Woman's Prophecy
trans. Henry Adams Bellows

To redeem those who lived in the past and to create all 'it was' into a
'thus, I willed it'—that alone should I call redemption.

Thus Spoke Zarathustra
trans. Walter Kaufmann

Contents

I
SIGURD

Magnus

They were going to clap me in jail as soon as the baby come. So I fit my fiddle into its sea-green case, tied up my worldly goods in my best noserag, and walked clear to the harbour ha to catch a ship, maybe forty steps from my father's house. She was a mail packet on her way to Bergen, space for sixty passengers. I waited in the trees along the quay till I was sure all were off who was getting off. No one had bought a ticket yet from Hans Uskedal, I'd checked at the ferry house to be sure. But you could bet all the folk who come down to poke their noses in other people's business wouldn't let me slip off, not without some parting scene at least of me with my mother weeping.

I wasn't going to blubber away with my chum Alf either, no matter how close him and me were from our first day at school. I watched him, slumped on his spine against the clapboard wall with the other boys, always having to be seen and not heard. Then I seen his lip twitch the way it did before some sarcastic remark. The joke took the rest by surprise, making them snort to try to hide it. A group of men with hands clasped at their rears turned to look down long noses at such scoffers. Skinny old Pastor Torsnes stalked away in disgust. What is the world coming to? his skull catechized the ground.

Alf's big ears stuck out even more for being so red. His eyes were on the ground too, hidden by the beak of his tweed cap. He was always a joker like me. But in that moment I seen him rooted to the spot, belonging right where he was. It was like I had slipped out of myself, looking back at some guy I used to be.

It scared the hell out of me, so far gone already I nearly missed the blame deck hands pulling the gangplank in. I had to run like blazes and jump the space just as they were casting off.

"Magnus Vangdal," a mean voice clapped at my behind, "if you run off, you'll be the death of your poor father."

It was our neighbour, Krist Oddnes, always forecasting the worst for me no matter what I did. I climbed over the rail and looked back. Alf and the others had flocked like gulls to the edge of the quay.

I know I give a pretty good imitation of Pastor Torsnes.

"Herr Oddnes, I forgot to tell you last time that the widow from Malkenes sent her regards to you. Should I tell her you'll come back soon?"

Old Krist looked so blame bare I could kick myself for missing the fun to come. Alf and the boys were snorting like horses rolling around in fresh pastures. It was just the old joke, why so many boat-builders liked to row their wares alone for sale in Bergen.

But Ola Uskedal was one boy who never got the joke, no use to start now.

"What will Gyda say?"

You'd think he'd understand more of the ways of this world with his father a ship agent.

"You tell me," I said over the widening water. "Since you know so much."

"They say her father will clap you in jail." Ola was tickled by the sound of it. That got the rest excited, screeching like gulls that wheeled around our ship. I could wish for a bit of garbage to toss at them.

Alf was the only one to keep his peace, knowing me better than the rest. The ship plowed the waves out into the harbour, as far as the walls of rock. A lot of rowboats were moored close to shore, bobbing like the heads of the old men. Only the fishing *jakt* rode calmly at anchor, the one boat meant for an open sea.

I picked out Alf's freckled face one more time, hoping he would do something to make me laugh. His eyes said they looked their last on me. I damn near bawled to think I could have asked him to tag along. Onsvik dropped away to a cluster of wooden houses beneath the mountain. I was still hunched over like a sucking babe, drinking it in.

"Ticket, please."

The purser's whiskers bristled like a housewife's broom. But he didn't know me from Adam.

"There wasn't time to get one. So many different ones come down to see me off."

He scowled. "You're not a runaway, are you?"

"I'm going to visit my uncle in Bergen."

He looked at me closely. "Then you should know enough to buy your passage on shore. I can only take your fare as far as Strandebarm."

As I fished in my trouser pocket, his stern eyes softened.

"Save yourself some money next time. Pay the whole fare in advance."

I didn't ask how much, scared to look any more dumb. Instead, I took a chance on a ten-*kroner* note.

He scowled more than ever, having to fish through his purse for a fistful of coins.

"Where does a boy like you get ten crowns?"

"Road-building." I straightened up with a man's pride in his work. "Vangdals *akkorden*. Maybe you heard of it. It's my father's contract."

His lip curled back under his great grey soupstrainer.

"So you're one of those who want roads to take the place of ferries, hey?"

I seen which way the wind was blowing.

"It won't be for awhile yet. We're stuck on the shoulder of the fjord halfway to Norheimsund. We'd have to bring down half the mountain just to get ten feet of ledge."

"It's God's will," he said with satisfaction.

The screw changed speed, shimmying the deckplates. It was almost like the earth quaking underfoot when we were blasting on the mountain. Thinking maybe this would be the time we broke through.

"Try drilling higher up there! We ought to profit from that crack. Careful now, tamping the dynamite! Everybody back? *Vær så god,*

13

let her go. Would you look at all that rubble? No, we're going to haul it for fill. Lean into those shovels now."

Really going nowhere. It was always just more rock hemming you in. In Amerika, no one cared what you did. Oh, my brothers pretended it was no different from here, writing how they went to the Lutheran church where the pastor ruled the roost. But they only did that to make my father feel better. When my mother found out I was gone, she would weep and pray, pray and weep, till I was glad to be free of such a hubbub. You might as well be dead as be a Lutheran. Gyda felt the same as me, she wanted to live all she could. I could tell what she wanted the first time I come home with her brother from that blasted road, snow on the ground in April yet. I never seen a girl so hungry for life. And me so dumb, I still hadn't figured out they come apart above the ankles.

Me and Selmer come into his yard after dark, the house lit like a lamp beneath us. We took off our heavy clothes in the outer hall, colder inside than out. Then we ducked through the kitchen door where a woodstove was roaring. I nearly landed on my face, catching my foot on the high sill. That bugger Selmer just laughed, never warning me it was half a foot high.

His mother spoke real sharp. I looked up to see her scowling at him, a plump-faced woman who couldn't stay mad if she tried. She smiled at me, wiping her hands on her clean apron, and come from the cupboard to take me by both hands. I liked her, the way she made such a fuss over me. My mother had taken to acting the same with all my brothers gone. Sigvald, the third one, had never made land again, dying of cholera in New York harbour because they wouldn't let anyone off the ship. That was before I knew the price of a mother's love.

Ha you bet I had it coming to me, such a damn fool kid I was not to see what Gyda's Mom was after. And here I thought Mrs Rogstad was always so jolly, ready to laugh at all my stories. I couldn't see one mean bone in her body, every bit as fat and merry as she seemed to be.

Gyda was another story, as different as night from day. The moment her mother called her from the front room, I wanted to kiss those pouty lips. She didn't talk much, except with her eyes, mostly just looking restless. Still she held my eye long enough to make it plain I could suck honey in there. I kept my eye on her too, much as I could while joshing her mother, but the flower was closed on the bee.

14

I should have guessed it would take more than a bee to scare so many town boys away. Oh, it was all such damn scheming it makes me sick. We never knew about them hypocrite town folk before the road come down to Onsvik. Even their gossip was lies, all those stories about me laying claim to big farm lands for my Dad, with pastures scattered high in the mountains. I might have talked a bit about our one poor *seter*, just a hut up there on top of the world, where I played the fiddle once or twice to some cows. The cows come lowing too like a herd of bassoons, begging to be milked, while I scraped and skirled, trying to make them skip to my tune. I told Gyda about it when she complained about so many eyes behind the curtains, waiting to judge. The town was as stuffy as the fjordwalls shutting us in.

Ha I was so damn busy sniffing out a place to go I couldn't see her folks blind to what went on under their noses. I never thought a thing when Selmer climbed up to the loft that first night to sleep, giving me his bedroom to use as I pleased. They liked me, they were only trying to make me feel at home.

Even Per Arne, Gyda's father, took a shine to me. I was tickled pink, that first Sunday morning, when he said to me and Selmer to come down and look at the boat he was making. Gyda looked disappointed when I said sure, but Aslaug, her mother, only smiled and said boatbuilding must be God's work too, or how could folk ever get across the fjord to church?

Ya, you bet I was slow compared to them. Per Arne took the hill down to the boatshed in about a half a dozen jumps. I could see Gyda getting some of her movements from him, neither of them able to sit still. The little stump had disappeared like a gnome when me and Selmer skidded in the open door.

It was pretty dim in there, what with grey clouds skimming the mountains beyond the freckled windows. But say, did it smell rich with pine shavings and sawdust drifted over the wide plank floor! There was a bunch of rowboats humped like whales back in the dark, and another ribbed skeleton under the dusty window. The little guy hopped over to a sharp-keeled craft shaped like a Viking ship. I wasn't far behind, reaching out to stroke the smooth white planks, soft as a girl's skin.

"You like wood?" Per Arne almost pounced on me.

"Ya," I said without a lie, "this would sure beat farming and fishing."

15

The little bantam didn't say another word.

"Dad's trying to get me to work with him," Selmer piped up. "He's scared of that road we're building. He thinks it will do away with rowboats. But you can't catch fish from a highway, hey Magnus? Besides, who wants to sit here every day watching the sun come up?"

"Not me," I said, stroking the flank of the boat's smooth bottom. Wasn't I the fish just begging to be caught? Per Arne led me through that side door to the vestry ha, a sweet little shop where a picture window looked out on the fjord. Fiddles hung like hams from the rafters, festooned with tiny painted flowers.

Per Arne seen me lick my lips. He reached for the scroll of the finest fiddle.

"I hear you can play," he said, tightening a bow. "See what you think of the tone." And he give up that shapely body into my shaky hands.

My quivering fingers made it hard for the music to skip. Once or twice I caught the bridge with the bow and made a terrible squawk. Per Arne and Selmer eyed one another and smiled. I felt too awkward to carry on. But while I was handing it over, I noticed the back and ribs of a half-finished fiddle on the bench. Beyond it was the table part with an f-hole already carved out.

"Do you make them yourself?" I whispered like a kid. Per Arne would have made me his partner too, if I'd become his son-in-law. But they all wanted it too bad, no other hope left for Gyda.

If things weren't happening so fast, I might have made out the drift. But Gyda was so scared I might get away to Amerika that I talked all the more about it. No one could say I didn't warn her. I just didn't count on getting that far on my third visit. Not with her folks sawing wood like that right down the hall.

The door opened and I was sure it was Selmer, his loft too cold for him this once. Then I heard all those clothes rustling, a waistband snap, and I said to myself, No you don't, you bugger, not with me you don't. I reared up and give him a mighty shove just as he leaned over me, naked as the dawn, and down he went with a gasp on the bare board floor. Ha, no wonder they put you in the loft, I thought, even your mother knows what a queer fish you are.

Gyda's little wail come up like a voice from the bottom of a well.

"Magnus," she quavered, "don't you want me like you said?"

I felt about as dumb as I have ever felt in my life.

"Gyda!" Then after a minute, "Is that you?"

"Ya," she said, but now she was staying right where she was.

"Aren't you cold?" I couldn't think what else to say.

"Ya," her voice was sort of ashamed. I pictured her the way she looked with all her clothes on, standing thin and pale under the pines, hugging her rabbit-trimmed sweater around her. For some crazy reason I asked, "Don't you have your glasses on?" I must have been all mixed up, my first time.

"I could see all right," she said stiff as a board. "It was you who hit me."

I give out a laugh before I could stifle it. She had to say "Shhhh!" for quite some time. Then somehow we were both giggling like girls, hugged tight together under the feather *dyne*. I run my hands over her terrible goosebumps, poor girl, still not able to believe it. Her long legs stretched nearly to my toes, fitting close as two planks on a ship. And then before I knew it, I was riding them waves, her heels hooked like anchors around my calves. Hell, there was nothing to it, I knew just what to do. But before I knew it I was slipped all the way up with nothing to stop me. It wasn't a busted drum, either, that made her moan like that, move like that. Jesus, I thought, don't move like that! I tried to back out quick, but she grabbed my ass and heaved and hissed like foam on the waves.

"Oh Magnus," she breathed into my spent neck, "I'm yours." But her muscles clutched like a fist, saying the opposite.

I pushed up on my elbows.

"You done this before," I said between my teeth.

She kept her trap shut.

"If you're up the stump, Gyda, it's not because of me."

Still I was trying to back out. She gripped me like a vise, then went limp as a rope, starting to cry. I rolled off, but she got so loud it was my turn to hush her up. Yet what could I do if she meant for us to get caught?

"I didn't mean it, Gyda. You just felt—you know—like you done it before. Wasn't there something I was supposed to break?"

She cried as hard as ever. So I was the one, white as driven snow, who would be made to take the blame for her dirt. Still I had to be so sweet and cute, like I would gladly be the goat.

She got quiet at last, or else I slept. She woke me with a kiss before she sneaked off to her room.

17

I left the next morning, filled with promises to come back real soon. But I wasn't going to set eyes on the troll king's daughter another night, not if it killed me.

She waited three months to make it look good. Then her Dad wrote mine to say it was my kid. Fat chance. Only my Dad wasn't the kind to listen to me before he took some stranger's word for it.

"Why don't you just kill me?" he said with the slit envelope still in his hands, hands so big they made the envelope itself look like a postage stamp.

"Whatever they say, it isn't true."

He stood like a stave cross over me.

"Don't you lie to me. You told them enough lies already. All the farms I'm supposed to have. Why don't you just kill me and be done with it?"

He staggered toward his bedroom. My mother looked at me as if he'd taken to his bed for the last time, I was his murderer.

I guess I spent the day in bed myself. I know that night I had an awful fever. Mother come up the stairs with ice-cold water in a basin. She wiped my brow with her cool hands. She prayed and pleaded with me.

"Your father can't live with your disgrace," she said. "Gyda will be a good wife to you. Marry her, Magnus. Don't let your father die."

I was the one dying with a fever, but nobody give a damn about me.

"Think of your little baby," she said again. "He'd be better off dead than to be born without a father."

I wished I was dead myself, and I had a father.

When I was finally out of my head with fever, Mother made me get down on my knees to pray with her. She said it was the words of King David after he got another man's wife with child. Why wasn't I the wronged husband then, that child none of mine? Still I couldn't say it without using the blame word *husband*.

At least her praying put me to sleep. Each time I woke up with the fever raging, she was there. She would lean forward and cool my forehead with her hand. I could hear her crying when she thought I'd drifted off to sleep again. Then she would pray out loud, thanking God for putting enough sorrow in my heart that I would say the sinner's prayer.

After breakfast, Dad huffed up the stairs to see me in my bed. He looked out the window at the humprock in the harbour, then down at me.

"Mom says you want to do what's right," he said real gruff. "I'll help you build a house on that piece of pasture up the mountain. I won't be going back to the road gang anyway."

He didn't wait for any answer from me, it was all decided. I guess he was a little ashamed to see me like this in bed. He ducked out as soon as his piece was said.

The roof stooped over me, I couldn't get out now, I was gasping for breath. They would all say, Don't do what Magnus did, you'll end up trapped like him. My life was as good as over. I might as well be dead, really dead, as to give them what they hoped for.

Still I didn't let on to my folks. The next day at breakfast my Dad said we were going back on the mountain to cut timber. He sliced the brown caramel cheese as if it was wood.

"But the boy has just had a fever," Mother said in a fearful voice. I think she was more scared of my father than anything.

"He's strong as an ox," Dad said roughly. So away went the ox to the woods.

The ox wasn't so dumb he didn't pretend to make up with Gyda. But I went myself to Norheimsund, circling through the trees, then down again into town when I'd got past Rogstad's place. I asked around at a couple of stores, hoping for some dope on Gyda. Nobody knew me, nobody wanted to say nothing. But a few young guys grinned and said something about a ram got out of the pasture down in Onsvik. I walked nine miles home thinking that would be the day they put me out to pasture, just let them try.

Dad looked like he was going to kill me, the day the letter come, threatening jail. His right hand went up, my mother shrieked. Then his face looked like it was blasted. He went back to his bedroom and shut the door. I bolted for the woods rather than look at my mother suffer.

Oh, there was lots to think about in the clearing we had made for a bridal house. I was hoping the clouds would lift over the fjord, letting me see the white top of *Folgefonn*. It would be a sign that a wedding offered a clean start after all. But the fog rolled down the slopes, shutting us in. I looked away down the fjord after that, trying to imagine Amerika. That's all I knew ha believing that in Amerika you could be free to start over again.

I hung around Onsvik just long enough for the mail boat to come in. Mom had gone across a meadow to a neighbour's house. She said, so mournful in the door, "They're preparing for the birth of a *married* girl's child." Dad was back on the mountain where I'd left him, felling pines. He was welcome to my share of any lumber I had cut.

As soon as it was safe, I made straight for my folks' bedroom. The carved lid of the rosewood box was in its place under the bed. I lifted it out and sat on the sagging tick, shuffling through *Amerika brevene*. There were letters from so many we didn't even know. Sioux City, Iowa. Rochester, Minnesota. Many had blue ribbons inside: Harald's calf FIRST PRIZE in Iowa State Fair; Solveig's piano GRAND PRIZE in grand music festival of St. Paul. It seemed like a land of prizes for young people. I didn't have to stay here and grow old before my time.

I whisked open the envelope of paper notes and counted out nearly four hundred *kroner*. Still I was scared it wasn't enough. I dug under the pile of letters, rummaging till I unearthed a handful of specie dollars.

The weirdest feeling come over me that I was being watched. I slammed the lid shut and looked up. Not a soul there. There was only those old pictures hung in horsecollar frames on the wall. I tried to stare back at my great-whiskered *bestefar* standing with his hand on a scowling woman's shoulder. The eyes followed me down beside the bed. I give the box a shove and run like all getout.

I got stopped in the porch, at least, before I waved my good fortune around. But as I stuffed my pockets with banknotes, I could feel all those eyes there inside like so many witnesses.

It was a crazy thing I did next. Before I went to collect my few things upstairs, I got a knife from the kitchen cupboard and made myself face those blame photographs. The eyes didn't flinch as I carved them out of the paper. I took my time trimming every hole, harder to do with old paintings where so many strings were left behind.

But it didn't help the way I thought it would. The blame eyes all seemed underfoot when I glanced back at Onsvik lying low on the water.

"*Takk for alt,*" I murmured over the ship's rail, mocking the pious words on every tombstone. But the old ones might thank me instead for opening a window onto my escape.

I watched over my shoulder the whole time the ship was docked at Strandebarm.

"You forgot your change," the ticket agent called behind me.

I was scared he had a telegraph message to nab me.

We crossed over the fjord at the head of Varalds Island, almost as green as me ha, before rock took over on the slope. Across the way, the mountains soared above Aenes, grey granite streaked with snow though fall shone bright as gold in our lower world. Then we were out of reach of telegraphs and I could think straight again. I'd forgot that ghosts stopped short at the water's edge.

When we steamed into Lokksund, I wished Alf was there to joke about the Malkenes widow. It was pretty tight in there, the cliffs like walls on either side. The captain plowed the wicked current, docking in a great thrashing of white water in the cove around the point. *Malkenes,* the sign on the ferry house said. There was one other building. No sign of any widow, just like I guessed.

We were still crisscrossing Bjørnafjorden when the sun went down. Lights come on in patches on the low slopes, far out across a sea where the fjord was almost lost. The distant mountains were disappointing, compared to the mighty shoulders of home.

More passengers were coming aboard than got off. There wasn't room any more to lie down on the bench. I had to sit and sleep with my neck against the wall. I kept my fists in my pockets to keep pickpockets out. It was a long night, stopping and starting. I dreamed once that my father was dead. After that I couldn't sleep. I stared at the dark islands, hardly seeing them pass.

The purser nodded when he come through, bawling that Bergen was next. I went on deck and stood right under the wheelhouse, watching the settlements thicken on the islands. Then we swung round a sharp bend and all of Bergen opened up inside the horns of a great bay, within the shadow of real mountains. It was beautiful till we got too close, houses of blue and red and yellow, all different and yet all familiar clapboard, long sheds like smears of paint along the waterfront. But when we docked at the ferry house, I had to crane my stiff neck to look at the rows of houses stacked above the harbour. It put me in mind of family portraits and I knew I hadn't come nearly far enough.

No sign at all in the terminal of a ship for Amerika. I hung around the wharves half the morning, scared to ask a soul. Finally I went up to a guy with a nose like mine, a real ski slope ha, who was ripping canvas from stacks of wooden boxes.

"Where's the ship for Amerika?" I sounded almost sure of myself.

"*København*," he said without looking at me. He seemed to be counting his crates. I waited. His cap was pushed back from a bare forehead, all the hair transplanted to a big brush on his lip. "There's no passenger service here," the brush jumped suddenly. "You'd have to go to Copenhagen or Hamburg. Unless you ship on a freighter from here."

His eyes dropped down to my fiddle case. "Maybe you'd hate to dirty them lily white hands, though."

"The Rockefellers are waiting for me to stay with them," I said cool as you please.

"Why didn't you say so? The boat they sent to fetch you just sailed."

At least I didn't feel so dumb when I found the sign myself for the *København* ferry. It was going to sail today at four. The next one didn't leave for three days.

"Are there beds to sleep?" I asked the ship agent. I was so hollow tired it was the first thing out of my mouth.

"Ya," the guy put on such airs, "it's not like your peasant huts."

I could have told him afterwards about his high and mighty berths. I had to share a room with three other guys. The socks on one of them smelled like the whole sheep. Another old bugger kept moaning how it was his first night away from his wife. When I asked why he didn't bring her along then, he sucked his gums and said she had to sleep with women in the next cabin. The last guy was skinny as Pastor Torsnes and shrank back on the top bunk like we meant to rob him.

I finally had to beat it up on deck, sitting half the night at a table by the window with just my fiddle case for company. Below Stord I got my last glimpse of Hardangerfjorden, the mountains soaring into the clouds.

The next thing I knew, I was looking through a bedroom window. I could actually feel the horsecollar frame around my neck. It was no dream, either. The ship was grazing a long row of houses, a few clumps of trees along the rock shelf. Somebody told me, when we were done scraping the shore, that now I'd seen Haugesund. But it was sad to see the coast shrink down like that, more bare with every passing mile.

I woke up staring at bright lights. The sign on the quay said *Stavanger.* I dozed. But when we sailed out, the coast was on the wrong side and I had this crazy hope we were turning back to Bergen. When the open sea rose under us, I could only wish we had. We were pitching from peak to trough, nothing to see any more but water swelling on every side of us. I went back below decks, only worse in our cabin with the goatcheese of feet. The old man started blubbering how he hoped to see his wife in heaven. I said from what I'd heard it would be men and women in different berths there too.

Later I was sorry when we got hit by the storm's main blast. I got so scared I was ready to pray like Jonah from the belly of the whale. I would do what everybody wanted, go home and marry Gyda and be a good son to my folks. But the ship staggered on, we were beating out the storm. And then I felt like a kid for spilling my guts out in wasted prayers. In time we rounded Lindesnes, less bad inside the South coast.

By afternoon we were steaming up the long, rocky inlet at Kristiansand, the channel smooth as my chin. I watched the lighthouse come by with all the fellow-feeling of a real old salt. But I was glad when they put off our crossing of the Skagerrak till past midnight. The winds, they said, would die down. I had the cabin all to myself, too. The smell of feet blew out the open porthole. The old guy and his wife had gone ashore, heaven enough for me. I went to sleep at once. Didn't even wake up when we got under way. In the morning, one of the deck hands pointed out the Swedish coast. It didn't look like much.

Copenhagen was another story. It was so huge! all them red roofs stepping back from the flat shore, spires and domes and such thrust up against a level grey sky.

Then the Sound closed in like a river between buildings.

I longed to open my eyes and find us back at Lokksund.

The crowd stampeded to the gangway. I hung back till the very last, scared of that mob down there shouting and grabbing.

When I seen a sign *Til Kristiana,* I bolted for it like the cow for the barn. Luckily I got lost, shivering in a cold wind. Finally I come to a small canal running out of the belly of the city. It was crowded with masts and fronted by a four-storey wall of houses. Only the roof-line dipped and jagged like a range of mountains. But then I seen the crosses in all those panes of windows, off-centre like the flag. It was only a wooden bar running up the sash to where the lintel crossed it, but it felt like a thousand windows looking cross-eyed at me.

I turned the other way.

Havngade it said on the corner of one building. To my left was a boat-shaped building on the quay. When I come past the prow of brown shingles, I seen a real boat easing into its berth. A few people stood in line.

"Is this the ship for Amerika?" I said to a harbour hand tying down the hawser.

"*Malmø*," the guy grunted.

I looked at him like a fool.

"*Sverige*," he said as if I was a post.

"I want to go to Amerika."

"Do you speak English?" His own speech was *riksmål*, though I could understand him well enough.

"No."

He shook his head. Deep worry lines appeared in his forehead, making me see how old he was.

"Go ahead. Don't let me stop you. You'll come back all the same. Maybe sooner than me."

He wouldn't say no more, but went about his business. He was too old, anyway, to hope for a different life.

The quay was already empty of passengers from Sweden.

A tall guy caught my eye on the gangplank. He walked like he was dragging a ball and chain, glancing back to see if anybody noticed. I felt I could trust him.

"Do you know the way to the ship for Amerika?" I said in my best *nynorsk*.

His face went white as if I'd struck him.

"What do you mean?" I think he spoke Swedish.

He glanced once over his shoulder like he couldn't help himself. It was me all over again at Strandebarm.

"I don't know how to go about booking passage. You looked like you might help."

He pulled a fine silver watch out of his waistcoat. Maybe it was his foreign *riksmål* that made his speech so careful.

"Ya, there's time to look into it today."

So I waited for him to tell some guy about his steamer trunks. I fidgeted with my hobo bundle, tightening the knot.

When he come back, he eyed my bundle.

"Are you sure you've got the money to get you to Amerika? I don't mean just the fare. You have to have money or some other prospects before they'll let you in."

"Don't worry about me," I said as if I knew all about it.

"Ya?" He looked a bit too eager. "Well, come along then."

We walked in silence over the cobblestone I had paced.

"You're running away, I take it," he said after a time. And looked down as if he could see clear through me.

"No more than you."

His laugh was like a bark. So I was right about his sneaking off the boat.

"What would make a kid like you run away from home?"

I blurted the first thing that come into my head.

"My mother died. I didn't want to stay and take charity. There's nothing here to hold me."

"I'm sorry," he murmured. Then, "Why would you have to take charity when you have funds to get you in the door to Amerika?"

"Ya," I played dumb, really playing for more time.

"Your mother—did she take any charity?"

I looked down the empty street, the Sound now empty too.

"Maybe you wouldn't call it charity. She cleaned house for different ones in our village." I pictured my last day at home. "She wasn't good enough to be invited to their bridal parties."

He seemed to be weighing the facts. I had somehow to account for my money, I could tell he was stuck on that.

"I'm not saying folks weren't good to us." There was that huge stack of lumber we had sawn that Dad would have to sell. "I worked for a farmer who had a sawmill. He let me take scraps for firewood. Sometimes I would sell it for scantling."

I couldn't shake his cold stare without turning the tables on him.

"You haven't said why you want to go to Amerika."

His mouth looked grim.

"My father has just died. He was a very rich man. But he wasted my inheritance. My mother and three sisters will be crushed by his debts. I had to sell my yacht to help them. Now I go to seek our fortune in Amerika."

25

My traitor fears helped turn the tables on me.

"There was a shorehand at your ferry who'd been to Amerika. He said I would be back before long."

For an instant the bony face glared like a deathshead.

"You stay in Europe and you'll lose your soul to them! They'll never let you be more than the son of that floor-scrubber!" He laughed his short dog laugh again. "Look at me! At my trial, the newspapers called me a *trolley*-man's son. A trolley-man's *son!* When I was the most prominent archaeology student in the university."

He saw the way I was looking at him.

"Well, you don't expect me to believe your lies about wood-gathering, do you? At least I can account for my money."

I might have confessed at once if he hadn't cut me off.

"Would you care to take an *akevitt* before we go on? You're a fellow who might listen to the truth for once. What do you say? Shall we stop at a saloon?"

"I don't know why I lied to you," I blubbered. I was having to trot to stay up with those long legs. "Maybe I was scared when you could tell so easy I was a runaway."

"Aren't you?"

"Ya," I said lamely, falling a little behind.

He turned with a frown.

"Why should that worry you? You knew as soon as you saw me that we were birds of a feather. Trust your instincts if you won't trust me. Just remember, you lied to me first."

Now that I could face him, I could face those cross-eyed windows too. We passed through a forest of masts, then ducked down a set of steps beneath tall double doors. There was a nameplate of brass in the smooth stone wall. The cellar door opened into a smoke-filled room, plenty of sailors milling about, some in navy blue.

We took a booth. As soon as the waiter served us, my friend raised his glass.

"To truth, then," he said in such a mournful way, he had to mean business.

We each had a thimble-full of *akevitt* and a mug of beer.

"Truth," I said. The *akevitt* was bitter but warming.

"My mother is dead," he confessed at once. "So are my sisters. After the death of my mother, I didn't care about anything any more. I wanted to become whatever it was in me to be. But there are too many rules for that here. They put me in prison for a year. No one believes in me now."

"They were going to put me in prison too," I said with trembling lips. "I stole my father's money and beat it before he found out."

But when I thought of them back there, Alf and my old cronies safe in our village, I couldn't stop my damn lips from quivering. My tears sprouted like new grass to think how the boy I had been was lost.

My friend give me a stern look.

"I guessed it was something like that." But before I could excuse myself, he said, "For heaven's sake, don't feel bad about it. You'll never be more than your father was without casting him off."

I shrugged. I couldn't say a thing for fear I would start howling. Being a man was just what I feared most to be.

"You're the first guy," I said at last with an effort to change the subject, "who ever told me lying was a good thing."

"I never claimed it was good," he answered with a mustache of foam on his lip. He looked even more morose with his lip that way. "What makes you think I told you the truth just now?" He sucked at his lip, more pained than ever if it was possible.

I didn't know what to say any more. Maybe I'd misunderstood him. He wasn't a kid, I could see that. He understood a lot more things than me. He drew himself up, as if making up his mind about something.

"Lying," he said very solemn, "is only another advantage people have, like wealth or birth. You use it with the same sense of obligation. You show people what it's possible for them to be."

We sipped our beers in silence. Over in a dark corner, a deep voice stuttered out a few loud bars of song. It would insist on several notes, then fall back uncertain.

"Alright," I give in to my preacher friend's stare, "I'll tell you what you want to know."

And I done my best to make him see the old ones glower in their horse-collar frames while I ransacked the treasure chest. But everything got turned around as I talked, I was stuck on a ledge below those faces peering down, one above the other, before they stretched out in a human chain to pull me up.

"I'm scared to let go of them," I quavered. "I'm scared I'll land smack in the pit."

But my friend only stared real gaunt till I began to feel like the cat that walked around the hot milk.

"What is it you want from me?" I said as if I didn't know.

Back in the corner, the loud guy was urging his scrap of a tune again. The man behind the bar looked our way and shook his head. The vocalist's face was hid by all the heads craning his way. My friend glanced about, kind of nervous. But when the quarrelsome noise fell back a little, he picked a worse quarrel with my story.

"You haven't said why they were going to put you in prison if you ran off before your father learned you stole his money."

"No?" I would have to tell him something like the truth to keep his good opinion. "It was a damn whore. She said the kid was mine when she was already up the stump. I didn't even know a girl's parts were so different before she slipped inside my feather *dyne.*"

He leaned forward with a look of triumph. At the same instant the singer staggered out of the corner, barely able to carry his tune. His mouth was no more than a clearing in that red bush of whiskers, cleared if at all by that thunderclap of voice. He lunged for the post and hung on, bellowing at the ceiling like a bull being butchered. Still he shut his eyes like he was crooning a lovely ballad. I shrunk down, scared to death he would need some small guy to pick on. My friend hunched forward, his head bent low.

Red Whiskers batted his eyes and lurched toward our table, his mouth a cave where blacksmiths hammered metal. I didn't look nowhere.

"Sigurdsen, you bastard!" the voice clamored overhead. "Where's my fucking money?" The words were slurred, but I think he said, "I'll sell your hide to the tanner, you swindler!"

I looked up to see my lanky friend hanging by the scruff of his neck from a thick red arm. I didn't stop to think but whisked out my fiddle and took up the ditty where the blacksmith left off. After two bars my friend landed like a cat on his feet.

Red Whiskers' head swayed like the bull about to charge. I turned his tune to a smart little jig, till his chin began to nod and his eyes lost their point. Sigurdsen dodged his grasp and was out the door in a trice. I was glad before I looked round the circle of doubting faces. Then I played for dear life while the bull danced over my grave.

Red Whiskers fell over a chair. Half a dozen sailors jumped him. In all the confusion I scooped up my stuff and run. But I cursed that

Sigurdsen for letting me hang out to dry. The eyes that had ringed me guessed I was his partner in crime.

I looked back once or twice in the street, no one coming yet. As I run down the side of the canal, I found myself still casting about for my friend. I hadn't even known how scared I was to be on my own till he took up with me. Then my heart leaped to see him come flying up the gangplank of a barque on the canal.

"This way," he panted.

We crossed the bridge over the canal. My knees banged my fiddle case like a drummer boy in retreat. The street bend round at last on a bridge over the Sound. Before it stood a huge brick palace with a central stone spire. Dragons twined their tails up the pole from every direction. But my lungs burned like dragon's breath.

"I got—to stop."

"I didn't mean to leave you like that," Sigurdsen panted. Still he kept his scarecrow expression.

"Ya," I could afford to be bitter, "I'm obliged for your concern. You were just going for a ride on your old yacht, was that it?"

He laughed that short bark.

"You don't think I would lie to you now, do you?"

"*Vaer så god*, who was that bull you left me to fight? Was he just some pocket you picked? What did you do to him before you went to jail?"

He looked like he had supped on vinegar.

"I don't mind saying you did a noble thing back there. Perhaps I can do something for you one day."

But I couldn't quit while I was ahead.

"Did you ask the bull how he was fixed for money before you took up with him?"

He give me a cold, white stare and turned on his heel. I was so scared he would dump me, I guess I must have lost my head.

"Mr Sigurdsen?" I blubbered, then broke down crying when he wouldn't stop. I was awful wrung out from that hasty concert.

He turned around at the sound of my need. Still his face was bone white.

"The name is Gerden. Carl Gerden," he clipped it off short.

"I thought he called you—"

"He was a drunk. I never saw the man before in my life."

I had to put away my doubts.

"Well, I didn't know your name at all. How was I supposed to know?"

He smiled sadly.

"Many thanks for the apology, Mr —?"

"Vangdal. Magnus."

"Well, Vangdal Magnus, do you still think I'm going to rob you if we travel to Amerika together?"

"No," I said real humble.

"Let's get a hansom, then," he took the lead, "and make up for lost time."

But to get to the ship we had to ride back through the sailors' quarter. Gerden was glum and curious by turn as we passed through the narrow streets.

"How did you know that girl was a whore?" he asked real abrupt.

"She was up the stump," I reminded him. But his look of triumph had changed to doubt since his scrape in the saloon.

"I was pure as the driven snow," I added lamely. "She knew all the ropes."

"What about your mother?" he shifted ground so fast he left me hanging again. "Couldn't she see your impurity just by looking at you?"

I figured it was easier to give him what he wanted. For good measure I threw in the business about praying at Mother's knee. He laughed his dog laugh when I spouted the words: "Behold, I was shapen in iniquity and in sin did my mother conceive me."

After that we rode more easily. I was glad I could make him laugh.

"Did you ever see your mother and father in sin?" he asked out of nowhere.

"No," I said taken aback, "did you?"

He only got real glum again. We rode in a strained silence. I figured maybe he was troubled by his mother's death.

"Were you close to your mother?" I said kindly.

"She had a difficult life. She watched nine daughters die of cramps. I hid the death of the last one from her, the one who was married in Amerika. My mother was very ill at the time herself and I lost her a few weeks later."

"I thought you said you had three sisters."

"Nine," he said real matter of fact. Then, as if to himself, "One by one, the muses have left me."

Mostly it sounded like a man trying on a new suit of clothes.

Before we could book passage on the *Helig Olaf,* we had to take a medical examination. We stood in an open hall, stripped to our shorts. Gerden had to draw attention from himself, it seemed, by leaving me naked.

"Did your mother pity you for what you did?" he said just before our line brought us up to the doctor.

"Ya, sure," I answered vaguely. I wasn't going to tell him in front of so many that she pitied my father more.

Then it wasn't his examination any more. The doctor studied my hands, looked down my throat and in my eyes. He asked me to drop my shorts, then lifted it with a short stick. I couldn't help myself. But he only nodded and wrote out my certificate. I figured maybe you had to keep it up if you wanted to last in Amerika.

We had to stand in another line yet to be questioned by a guy Gerden said was a Consul. I was worried what he might ask.

"Did your mother—" Gerden started to say when I turned on him.

"What's the use of casting off my father if you're going to hound me all the time about my mother? I thought you told me to be the man I wanted to be."

Faces in line were starting to turn. Gerden looked like he seen a ghost. I waited for him to bolt. But I didn't care, some prices were too high to pay. He surprised me by nodding, though he looked away pretty grim.

The Consul wanted to know how much money I had. I figured it was best to empty my pockets. I seen Gerden's eyes trying to count it. My doubts began to get the best of me again. The Consul looked at me with suspicion.

"What are you going to do in Amerika?" He was very stern.

With my heart in my mouth I said, "I will live with my brother in Minnesota."

"Where in Minnesota?"

I could only remember Harald's calf FIRST PRIZE and Solveig's piano. But which was in Minnesota?

"St Paul." I had a horrible, slipping sensation. But the guy nodded and let me go.

At the ticket counter I asked the cheapest way.

31

"Two second class fares, please," Gerden interrupted.

I was dumfounded. "I have to save for—"

"I want to pay the difference," he said very delicately. "I owe you that much."

I was ashamed to be so suspicious. But I couldn't forget his eyes lighting on my money.

"Don't think you can buy any more dirt about me. I'm leaving that kid behind."

He shamed me, then, with his cool politeness.

"Don't assume I'd remain in your debt either. The past is forgotten the moment we set foot on that ship."

So we sailed the next day in a second class cabin. We both had to run the gauntlet of shower rooms and doctors' needles, before our baggage was fumigated. Some guy even come along and sprayed us with a strong-smelling drizzle.

"It's so good to be pure again," I said before I thought.

"If you'd sailed steerage," Gerden said sourly, "they'd have sprayed you with a firehose."

It was the only time he put my face in it. I couldn't complain.

It wasn't much fun, though, to be cooped up in a stateroom with him. His face was whiter than the milky walls. Mostly he moped on his bed or brooded out the porthole. He wouldn't look at me. I got the feeling I should make myself scarce. He didn't like to have me so close on top of him. He found there wasn't room for tomorrow with me reminding him of yesterday.

I went on deck to look again at a world I should have turned my back on. In the neck of water off Helsingør, I watched a ferry ply its way to Sweden. My stomach churned like its white wake.

That night I done my best to sit through Gerden's kind of concert in the forward lounge. The stuffed chairs weren't so hard to take as that blame funeral music. I kept watching the fiddlers in hope of a cheery note. But they sawed away with their noses in their sheet music like they were scared to death to strike out on their own.

Then I found out about the real concerts going on in steerage when I went down to see what it was like. It was terrible crowded, several huge compartments holding a hundred double bunks—not like our snug little cabin with twin beds and chairs. But the music was what folk played for themselves. It was mostly Galicians, round women with kerchiefs tied over their heads, men in leather boots

rumpled below their knees like stockings, and kids, lots of kids.
I heard the music, then caught a glimpse of a concertina flash like
a mermaid's ass. There was a whole bunch of players seated in a
square between the bunks. The mandolin player grinned when I
kicked up my heels a little. Then the women clapped hands and the
band got real lively.

I clapped loudest of all when the song was done.

Still there was little I could say to all those foreign sounds on every
side, so many *ch*'s and *k*'s. We bobbed and nodded, more helpless
now than me and Gerden to use words for fun. Then a guy held out
his fiddle for me to try.

I struck up an old Hardanger tune, soon caught by all and played
as merry as you please. The bare-handed fiddler never took his
shining eyes off mine.

"*Dobre, dobre!*" so many cried when we came back to earth. I
knew it was *godt* in any language.

It was hard to explain that I meant to go up and get my own fiddle.
I pointed overhead, pretending to play. They all smiled and shook
their heads. But when I turned to go, hands prevented me.

"Oh," I caught on at last, "you're not allowed up on our deck, is
that it?"

They looked at me dumb. I traced a finger down the companionway, pretending to play.

"*Dobre,*" they laughed, "*dobre.*"

But the shoe was on the other foot when I seen Gerden on his
bunk. His eyes reminded me of a caged dog.

"Why don't you come down to steerage with me?" I took pity on
him. "There's a bunch asking me to play with them."

He raised himself on an elbow, looking down his nose like a
carpenter sighting down a rafter.

"I didn't pay second class to slum with a lot of Galicians."

"Oh come on, Carl. You said yourself we had to leave the old ways
behind. Come down a little in the world and have a good time."

"You go enjoy yourself," he said so nice I didn't have the heart to
leave him now. Not when he'd turned back like that for me.

"Let's go to the saloon instead."

We stood at the long bar. There wasn't a drunkard in sight. I
wished we could pick up at that moment before he thought he
looked bad in my eyes.

"I haven't told you the best part about my mother."

He didn't move an eyebrow.

"Don't feel you have to lie to me. You owe me nothing."

When I tried to say I owed him quite a lot, he cut me off.

"No, you caught me in a contradiction. We have to leave our past lives entirely behind."

His hatred of high mucky-mucks seemed a bigger contradiction when he wanted to be one himself. But I took my cue from him.

"To the future," I raised my glass. "To the men we're going to be."

"To the future," he agreed.

We couldn't seem to imagine it. We talked instead about how glad we were the day before yesterday to watch the coast of Jylland sink beneath the waves.

The next day I went back to the Galicians. They welcomed me with open arms. There was beer here too, frothy stuff that lent its head to your heels. I got to know so many songs by heart that one guy pulled on a woman's shawl and baptized me with a half a bottle of beer. Women lined up to kiss my streaming lips.

Gerden asked me at dinner how life was going in the depths.

"But then," he said with cold eyes, "you're used to hanging from the bottom rung, aren't you."

"Let me pay you back," I said stung, "for my second class passage."

"I never buy myself companions," he sneered. "I like to keep my creditors at a distance too. But they're easily bought off, as you can see."

I looked steady at him while I filled my pockets with good bread. Then I wrapped some sliced beef inside my jacket.

"The company's better down there. I don't see why the meals shouldn't be a little better too."

But the last day before we touched at Halifax, Amerika, I quit the concert early. I hadn't been fair to Gerden. At least he wasn't cooped up inside the cabin like I feared. I found him in the bar with his back to me. The bartender was looking down in the sink.

"No, it's me," Carl was saying, "who's a Hardanger man. The other guy's a German named Gerden."

I ducked out before they could spy me. I went and sat a long time in the companionway. I thought I could see after awhile what he was up to. He wasn't very happy with himself. He was welcome to try my

34

boots if they would help. Most likely he'd want to be quit of me entirely then. He would probably sneak away at Halifax. I could only wish him well for what he'd tried to do for me.

All the same I hated to let him go without some kind word. I know I let Alf down by leaving the way I did.

That night we were lying in our beds, Gerden reading as usual before he put out his light. I looked across the little space.

"Carl, I'm sorry I let you down."

He looked up startled. But he was too stiff to ask any more.

"What I mean is, I didn't turn out the way you expected. I give you the wrong idea, I guess. I really can't be comfortable anywhere but the bottom. You went to good schools. You don't have to be a trolley man's son. You showed me I don't have to be a farmer's son, either. But I'm a farm boy all the same. I don't want to change that."

It was quite a speech for me. I was always glad I made it.

Gerden smiled his dog grimace.

"You should do well enough in Amerika."

"If I do, it will be partly your doing."

"*Ja, takk.*" His lips thanked me but his eyes didn't believe me. I guess he never knew I told him he was going.

I watched him go away the next morning on a dock glistening with rain. I waited by the lifeboat till he disappeared around a wall of luggage. The stevedores were still wheeling steamer trunks out of the hold.

I scanned the low, wooded hills around the long harbour. It made me bleak to think I might have stayed back in Bergen.

We were well out to sea before I found my fiddle was missing. At first I couldn't believe it. I looked high and low, crawling clear under both beds. But that bastard Gerden must have spirited it away somehow, maybe give it to a stevedore in case I seen him.

Sigurdsen, my mind said too late, not *Gerden,* you dope. Didn't Red Whiskers try to warn you?

Maybe he would even make his money back by selling my pet fiddle. But I knew it wasn't just the money. The bugger took away my music, took it away because it was the only way I could talk to my Galician friends. And he did it for nothing but spite. Now the peacock couldn't even explain how he lost his tail.

I got so I kept to my stateroom between meals, a regular Gerden myself. *Sigurdsen,* I kept thinking. Well, why not? I couldn't rest. In the morning, when the steward knocked to say New York was near, I grabbed up my bundle and never looked back.

I was right by the rail when we steamed under the Statue of Liberty. A man told his wife in Swedish it was the tomb of Columbus. But the sight of that waiting woman in a nightgown convinced me it wasn't true. I was so big with thoughts of liberty, I had to stand rammed against the rail so I wouldn't show.

I waited for the crowd at the gangplank to thin out a little. As we come down the steps, my heart sank to see police stopping everybody. But they were only tagging us with a number, nine on every breast pocket.

We were herded straight toward waiting ferries. I looked with sheep's eyes at the forest of tall buildings across the water. I could feel smug at last, so easy to get in.

But the ferry made for an island square as a box. It was all red brick buildings, hardly a yard of earth to be seen. A regular brick shithouse stood over all, topped by four onion towers. Then I seen the light. I wasn't in yet.

We were let off in a ferryslip that nearly split the island in two. I followed an old Galician couple, each carrying a wicker basket. I couldn't see any of the ones I knew. I hoisted my bundle over my shoulder, one finger in the knot, feeling the knot in my gut tighten.

We streamed under the girdered canopy into the fortress. The iron stairs echoed with the dull ring of feet. The old man and woman huffed and puffed in front of me. At the top, some guy in uniform took them aside. Their faces were grey as dough. Then I seen wire cages where people huddled inside like animals, trying to look as if they had nothing to fear.

The crowd pressed me into one of the runs between handrails of pipe. We were in a great, high hall, and the lineups went on forever.

Too soon our line come up to a man who peeled eyelids back with a steel buttonhook. I could feel his breath in my face as he rummaged out of sight. At first I saw red, such an awful hurt.

"God," I thought he said. Then he jerked his head. "God on."

He wiped his buttonhook on a towel and bent down to pry another set of lids.

The man in front of me carried all his papers in his mouth. His arms drooped with boxes held by string.

"Baransky?" the official read the name on the papers.

36

I tried to understand what was going on.

"Poland?"

The old man nodded at the name, the woman too. He asked them a lot of questions in Galician. I could only hope he spoke my language too.

Baransky and his wife took up their boxes and moved on.

"_____," the guy in uniform said in a bored voice.

I took a chance on what was asked.

"Sigurdsen," I said, my heart racing.

He took a look at my papers. He was shaven, still his face was so dark it appeared dirty.

"_____?"

"Eg snakker ikke engelsk."

He give me a blank look. His cheekbones were sharp enough to puncture my lies.

"Spell it," he said.

I shrugged.

"_____," he smiled. Then he said, "John Smith," writing it on the papers I had given him.

I shrugged.

"De heter John Smith," he said with a grin.

It was the grin that made me mad.

"Nei, I are Magnus Sigurdsen."

"_____ Denmark, John Smith?"

"Norge," I said helplessly. The pencil paused, the guy looked at me again. "Nor-vay," I tried to remember the English word, pretty sure he understood my Norwegian.

He acted out counting money. I took the roll out of my trousers, aware of his greedy eyes. So I peeled off 20 *kroner,* thinking it was what he wanted. He only laughed and stamped my papers.

"You can go."

I stood there, not sure if he was mocking me still. Then I had to keep myself from wringing his hand.

"Mange takk. Mange, mange takk."

A ferry boat stood well out in the Sound beneath that forest of tall buildings. I watched its track open wide like a plating of silver. Before the streets of gold.

It didn't really matter who I was. I might turn out to be John Smith. I might be anybody I chose to be.

The crowd pushed through the ferryshed onto the waiting boat. There was a great rattle of chains and we edged away from the wet plank wall of the slip. I watched the city grow up around us as we crept toward the foot of the land. There were two great towers, twenty storeys or more, that made me think of the houses in Bergen all looking down from on high.

It didn't make no difference, though, when I did steer clear of that side of town. I stuck to the east side where I could smell salt water. I didn't feel so cooped up here, plenty of empty spaces between the buildings, weeds growing high on every lot. The street was paved in places with dirt and broken stone.

People turned to stare as I went by, a guy like me in such a funny suit. Little children pointed, not like at home where only your elders could judge. I flopped along like a fish out of water, looking neither to left nor right.

"What's your hurry?" The voice at my shoulder spoke in *nynorsk*.

I swung round, closing my fist. It was only a young guy like me, short and burly in a thick white sweater, but with the biggest head I ever seen. His hair curled tight as a mop thrown over his head. He looked way too old for his years, probably that pumpkin head, much bigger than his fat ass. He smiled, big gaps in his teeth.

"Are you just come from home?" He eyed my hobo bundle, then the cut of my suit.

"Ya," I said, still suspicious. I wasn't one to be taken in twice by strangers.

"Do you know where you're going?"

I made no sign, just kept on walking.

"It's hard for the new ones here," he said sadly. "It's hard enough for us old ones too. I'd be glad to help you just to get the latest news from home."

He said *eg*, not *jeg* like the ones from Kristiana or Copenhagen. I felt my tide of suspicions go out.

"How long have you been here, then?"

"Two years," he said sadly. He didn't look a day older than me, except for that huge head. "It's no place for foreigners. I'd go home if I could get the fare."

I thought of my two hundred plus *kroner* in my pocket, fingering it lightly to be sure.

"Martin Ness is my name," the guy said. He stopped and faced me squarely, holding out his hand.

"*Eg heter* Magnus Sigurdsen."

"You're from Hardanger, aren't you?"

I looked at him in fright.

"Don't worry. I'm from Voss myself. I recognized your dialect."

My heart warmed right up to him. I felt at home, only free to do as I wanted.

"Do you have a place to stay tonight?" Martin tilted his huge head till he looked like he'd go right over. "Stay with me then. I got lots of room."

I blinked back a tear. He took my bundle, nodding his mop for me to follow.

On the way he proposed a drink to warm us up. It wasn't every day, he said, that he run into a Norwegian right off the boat. It looked to me like Gerden all over again, but I would go along with him till I found out what he wanted.

Martin asked what work I did at home.

I said, "Oh, odd jobs now and then. I applied to be King when the job was first open."

"You're a real card," he laughed.

I wasn't quite sure what he meant, a new expression to me. He might be inviting me to gamble. But I was safe from temptation.

We turned into a real joint he knew. He said not to mind the dirt on the floor, the drinks were cheap. It was dark but warm inside. We sat in a corner. He took the seat with his back to the wall. I thought he must be looking for somebody, the way he glanced around while I talked. Gerden, I said to myself, and told less of the truth. He asked me some more about Onsvik, then his eyes went their own way again.

"I know some Norwegian girls," he finally said with an owl's wise smile. "We could have a good time."

"Ya?" I grinned back, thinking Amerika was maybe a land of opportunity after all.

"They live at the boarding house next to mine. Come on, let's see if we can catch them at home."

We had to ride a yellow street-car to another ferry. I was colder now than before, I wished we had stayed inside.

"This girl I know is named Ottilee," Martin said with his back against the rail of the ferry. "She knows which side her bread is buttered on."

We rammed into the ferryslip a little too hard, cracking the planking. I asked was the captain coming too? Martin just laughed and took me by the sleeve out to a wide avenue.

The building we stopped in front of was five storeys tall.

"We're climbing right to the top," Martin said with his chest stuck out. "Think you're up to it?"

I looked at his stumpy legs and decided to be quiet.

In the stairwell, he looked at me sideways and said, "You got some jack, don't you? These girls aren't bad. But they got to eat."

I held onto the varnished rail.

"We're going to hooers, is that it? So you're a goddamn pimp."

I wasn't hurt to think he was after my money. I was hurt that no one ever meant to be friends. Alf had been my friend, I hadn't meant to run off on him.

Martin looked so blame hurt you'd have thought I was taking advantage of him.

"I bought you a beer, didn't I? And I've offered to share some girls I know. I even invited you home with me. You sure are slow to learn the ropes, even for a newcomer."

He turned back on the stairs, shrugging like I wasn't worth the trouble.

It was my turn to catch at his sleeve.

"I'm sorry," I said.

"Look," Martin blinked at me with those hazel-ringed eyes, cold as an owl's, "I do get sailors for these two girls. You're right about that. But if you're looking for work, you're not going to find much else right now. Times are bad here, have been all this year. I'd hate to see a fellow *Hordaland* man starve this coming winter."

I must have looked flabbergasted.

"Tell me what else you can go to work at without no training and no English." He give me a gaping grin. "Can't you see I'm taking you for your first job interview? If Ottilee takes to you, you won't freeze your ass off this coming winter."

The thought of any woman, even a hooer, waiting for me give me a prod on the spine. Hell, what difference did it make if I wasn't going to buy it? She wouldn't have to know I would never pimp. A little fun couldn't hurt no one so long as I kept my eyes open.

"Good man," Martin clapped me on the shoulder. And we took the rest of them stairs two at a time.

The girl who answered the door was puffy-eyed with sleep. Her nose was broad and flat, but her lips were full and red. Her hair was her best feature, piled up like spun gold.

"_____," she said in a brisk tone.

"He's *norske* too," Martin said. "Get in, Magnus. Were you born in a barn?"

I was too much of a sheep to say anything.

"This is Cecelie," Martin's voice warned me off from her.

She nodded without looking at me. The room was mostly bare, two wooden chairs, a hot plate on a low cupboard, and a brassposter bed in the middle of the floor.

Martin crossed the bare wooden floor to another door.

"Ottilee," he said, "I brought a friend for you." Then to me, "Go right in. That way she won't have to catch cold."

He almost pushed me through the damn door. It was already dusk, the blind drawn.

"*God dag,*" I said into the gloom. I wanted to see what kind of troll she was they couldn't show to the light of day. I kept one hand on the doorknob behind me, aware of my danger.

"*God dag,*" a quiet voice said from under the covers. "Was that Martin who brought you?" She coughed as if knives clashed inside her chest.

"Ya," I said. "Are you sick?"

"Just a cold. I hate to get chilled."

I kept my back to the door. Martin would be listening on the other side, sure to block my way.

"If you're afraid of Martin coming in," the voice read my mind, "there's a key here on the chair to lock the door."

"What am I supposed to—" I was going to say *pay you*. Instead I said, "I never done this before."

I heard her groan.

"I mean I never paid for it before," I tried not to sound like such a kid. "How much is it?"

"Two dollars," she sounded ashamed. "Didn't Martin—?"

"No," I said in embarrassment. Then after a time, "How much is that in *kroner*?"

A real sob come from the bed.

41

"Did I say something wrong?"

"No," her voice quavered. She sniffed for awhile. "I was remembering when I was just off the boat, still a good girl." She groaned, though not so sad now. "Come lie with me," she coaxed.

I could tell she was hungry for the way I still seemed so pure. But I was nobody's fool. I got the key first and stuck it right through the keyhole. Whatever eye had been watching pulled away in a hurry. Then I shot the bolt and left the keytip in to keep Martin from peeping. My trousers hit the floor as quick as my bundle.

"I don't like it with your shirt on," she said so tender that I flung right up to tear it off.

It was good in the dark, not having to see who she was, and I let my mind go. She was well-shaped, all her parts in the right place.

Afterwards I lay with my brain coming clear again, thinking nothing of it when she said she had to go to the bathroom.

"We'll lie and talk," she sounded almost loving. "Oh, how you take me back *home*, Magnus! Just let me check to be sure I don't get pregnant."

The springs squeaked, I squinted trying to see her naked. She went through the bathroom door and closed it. I seen the light shine under the door.

After five minutes I thought I better check. I was a real gentleman ha, I even knocked. The bathroom was empty, a second door gaping wide to the front room! The birds were flown. Except for one dumb pigeon.

I made a bee-line for my suit of clothes on the chair, already guessing it would be gone, nearly two hundred *kroner*. The suit was gone, even the change of shirt in my hobo bundle. Oh, I was too numb to cry, not a stitch to hide myself nor tongue to tell what had been done to me. Maybe it was just as well. The cops would want to know what I'd been doing in a hooer joint.

I didn't dare think for a time, nothing to do but look for any rag to cover myself. There was a closet in Ottilee's room, bare as my ass. I think it began to sink in how the girls lived somewhere else. Well, they could afford to stay away from this dump for a year if they wanted. Go to work clear across town.

I got a sheet from the bed to stop my damn shivering. There was only a tattered housecoat in the closet in the front room. *"Nammen,"* I heard my voice scolding, "you're not going to go out in public dressed like a hooer."

I peeped into the hallway, coast clear. I run out then as far as the bannister, praying I would see my monkey suit. The railing spiralled five storeys to the bottom. I looked away. After a minute, I skinned down one flight, then another, hoping to find my clothes in a heap in the landing. But Martin knew what he was doing.

I went up at last, lonesomer than a ghost. I had to stay back from the top bannister, it made me so dizzy.

There was nothing to do now but hide out in that damn pink rag. It hung a little below my knees, no belt to hold it together. I wrapped my arms around myself, bracing to spend a night in that bed where the sheep was shorn.

I tried my best not to think, but when I slept I saw my father's face, not angry at all, only searching my eyes with a look past speech. I woke up once when I thought I heard someone. But it was only some drunks in the street below, I could see them teetering and shoving in the lamplight.

Come morning it was my stomach that was the first thing to be heard. I looked out the window at the painted sign in *norsk*, Lutheran something or other. At least it beat going door to door in this building.

Down in the street I had to dodge a coal wagon and my robe flapped open. My bare feet felt as if they were stepping on hot coals.

The flag of *Norge* hung limp over the door the way it did at home the day I was confirmed. At least the door was unlocked.

I was doing myself up inside when a woman spoke from behind a desk.

"You're not a runaway, are you, son?"

"*Nei.*" And I give her a look that said I was at her mercy.

She did her best to spare me more shame. But she seemed to know just what wickedness had ensnared me.

"They've robbed you, haven't they?" she said wearily. "And you so young to be abusing your soul that way. Never mind," she took heart at some private thought, "Sister Hanstein will be glad to see you. But I expect you'd like a pair of trousers before that."

It turned out to be a hospital for poor Norwegians. The grey-haired Sister led me to a room with a cot and a washstand in the corner.

"I expect you'd like some breakfast too." She didn't wait for an answer. "You can try for now to make yourself decent with this nightshirt. Get into bed and I'll bring you a bite to eat."

43

She was away a long time, likely having to do the cooking herself. A spare woman in a black dress, spectacles dangling on her bosom, come in the door. I guessed it must be Sister Hanstein. I couldn't look her in the face. She sat in a chair by my bed.

"Poor child," she said feeling my forehead. "You have been to hell already, and so young. But surely you don't want to stay there, do you? Surely you still believe in Christ's mercy?"

When I didn't answer, she said more slowly, "How did you come to leave home so young? Oh, it's plain as the nose on your face you're a new arrival."

The way she said *home* made me long for Norway. But I wouldn't let her take any advantage.

"I was tired of being bullied by the pastor. I wanted to be free to think for myself."

"And do you like what you found," she glanced at the housecoat crumpled at the foot of my cot, "thinking for yourself?"

My pride was like a sandbank collapsing.

"We all need others," Sister Hanstein touched my arm. "God needs to show His love for us. I prayed God to send me someone in need today, someone He really wanted me to see. And I'm sure He arranged this meeting with you."

Her words were like the tide carrying out my poor sand. I had nothing to hold back the tears with no more, I could taste salt at the corners of my mouth.

"My child, my poor dear child," she said with such love and pity that I thought my heart would break. I saw my own dear mother again, leaning over my bed, and I prayed I might see her just once before I was lost forever.

Sister Hanstein talked till the other one come with the breakfast tray. When she heard about my brothers, she thought it would be best for me to go there at once. She didn't have to tell me to get out of this terrible city.

"Here," she said before she left, "I've written down my address. I'm sorry I don't have money for the train fare clear to Minnesota. God hasn't supplied your need that far. But there's enough here to take you to Buffalo, I think. You might work your way from there by lake boats. Now if you're ever in trouble again, you must come to me, or write to me, and I will help. Be sure now. God bless, my child. God be with you."

I left that city of hooers the same day, wearing coarse woolens that Sister Everson had found for me, and riding on a fish wagon. I prayed the psalm of David after he had gone into Bath-sheba, what I could remember from reciting it for Gerden. I could even forgive him for nagging all the time about mothers.

The fish guy wheeled onto Brooklyn Bridge. What a grand thing it was, like the hand of mercy let down from heaven itself! I whistled the fish man's tune with him while our horses walked across the water. When he pointed me toward Grand Central Station, I said, "God bless you. I won't forget you."

The side-street was thronged by sellers and buyers and gawkers like me. I bumped into a guy balancing a push cart. When he turned and yelled at me, I forgive him in my heart. But that fish guy knew what he was doing sticking to the broad way.

Later that day, watching through the window of the train where mountains loomed in the distance, I imagined God looking down from on high. "Why should He forgive me?" I thought. I couldn't have stood it if He did, having to feel so goddamn gracious like Sister Hanstein. I stretched my feet out on the wooden seat and tried to enjoy my misery.

The hiring hall was hard to find in Buffalo. I got turned around coming out of the train station the next morning, snow flying like sand in the stinging wind. I flagged down a few passersby who shrugged at my *norsk* confusion. Then I remembered the word baat, same in English as Norwegian, and I kept baying like the boat lost in a fog. A tall man in a fine black coat steered me straight in the end, scared I would run aground on him.

The Lake Carriers' Hall was one long windowless room. I stamped the snow off my feet at the door, looking around. There was only one guy in the place, sitting with his head in his hands. A row of empty wooden chairs lined each wall. The fellow didn't look up when I sat down two chairs away. He was so fair his hair was dirty white, eyebrows barely showing against his pale skin. His hands had puffed his mouth out some, making his nose and chin look like they were carved out of soap. He stared at the floor in such gloom I thought he'd be *norske* for sure. Or at least *svenske*.

"Were you the only survivor?" I kidded him, refusing to be ignored.

"They beat you up too, eh?" He didn't raise his head, but his cheeks turned red like he was ashamed.

45

"Who'd like to try?"

He was sitting up now, his fingerprints like snow on his cheek. He licked his thick lips.

"How did you get in here anyway?"

"The door was open. I—"

"Shit!" he said under his breath, then laughed. "I must have give as good as I got if they went home. Well, that should teach me to try slipping in after dark."

"It's snowing," I apologized like it was my fault.

"Ha," he said humourlessly. "Who but a dumb Norwegian would storm the gates after shipping season was over. No offense."

I liked him for not taking himself too serious.

"Ya, I been doing lots dumber than that."

He give me a grateful smile.

"I'm Gust. Hetland. You been over long? Your *norsk* isn't like so many talk here."

"I been in Brooklyn for awhile."

"Sailing the coast?"

"Ya."

"What's it like? Sometimes I've thought of doing it for the winter."

"I got tired of it," was all I could say.

"Did they promise you better wages here for strikebreaking?"

"Ya."

He let it go at that.

"Is the season really over?" I said after a time.

"A few always run until freeze-up. Sometimes they get caught in the ice-pack through the Soo." He wet his ruby lips, the only colour showing on him. "They put my boat into drydock last night after the ore was off. I was the only one going back to Duluth anyway. The whole crew was nothing but a tribe of Italians. Strikebreakers going to the Old Country for the winter. They all got wages on their passage over here. You never seen guys hated like those guys were."

"I guess I missed the boat," I tried to joke. But I was beginning to sweat, thinking how would I ever get to my brother's place without a *krone* to my name? I was a fool to take Sister Hanstein's word for it. What would a woman like her know about business in Amerika?

"Something is bound to turn up," Gust. saw the look on my face. "If you can stand going to hell in an ice bucket."

"Hell wouldn't be so bad compared to this place."

I meant it to be funny but the words come out sounding so blame sorry for myself. I was relieved when he didn't see his advantage. Then he was glummer than me.

"You should have seen us this last trip. We were iced up enough just to keep us afloat. It's that fog frost that starts to build up. You can't see more than a few feet. If hell is where you're cut off from hope, that's where we were."

"But you come back all right," I tried to steer him straight.

"Oh ya. We only stood a few feet out of the water when the blast hit us this time. Sometimes a north-east wind like that will stand a ship right on end. Then it's down to the bottom without time to get a lifeboat over. They said below it looked like the first wave washed me over. But I hung on better than the oak moulding that was ripped off the rail."

"That's a real storm," I done my best to sound devil-may-care.

"Ya," he sat up a little straighter, "but I guess you seen worse on the Atlantic."

He was such a babe I felt like a heel for doubting him.

"*Nei,*" I quit pretending, "we never had it as bad as that."

"You should have seen our pilothouse," he could be proud now of his fear. "It was hooded just like an igloo. The whole deck was frozen over in the shape of the waves as they hit. After awhile the pilothouse sent someone down on a line to have us chop ice so the wheelsman could see. I guess that's the life of a lake lookout, though. You can bet I'm moving up to wheelsman, and soon too. I can hardly face the thought of going ice-fishing this winter."

The way he laughed, he was a better man than me, dangling over hell on a lifeline.

"You should have seen me blubber my first time in a storm. Like Jonah in the belly of the whale."

Only I made it sound as if it had been years ago, and I was one of the boys who fished on the *jakts* all the way up to *Nordkapp.* He hooted at different sketches of my shipmates, like the guy with goatcheese in his socks. So I threw in Alf and so many back home, how we always had to get around those pinched noses. Only I didn't say beans about Gyda, scared to put myself in too bad a light.

We were still gabbing like cronies when an old coot come in, nose sharp as a cheese slicer.

47

"_____"

He might have been talking to the wall for all he looked at us. Still there seemed to be a lamp inside his eyes, they burned so bright. I got to my feet, Gust. not far behind me.

"_____," Gust. said. Then in *norsk* of a sort, "My friend only speaks Norwegian."

The old guy's dab of white beard was like a bib stuck to his chin. It quivered every time he moved his bottom lip.

"I need two able-bodied seamen," his eyes lighted on me like dry tinder.

Gust. was tugging at something in his coat pocket.

"Don't you have a discharge book?" he whispered to me as the captain leafed through the pages of Gust.'s book.

I shook my head.

"Where's his?" the captain didn't look at me.

"He was brought over as a strikebreaker," Gust. answered. His face bloomed, all one colour with his lips.

The captain only muttered, "I expect he'll do," and sucked at that mat of bib under his lip. "Has either one of you had any experience at the wheel?"

I could see Gust. was about to lose his chance.

"He has," I said real brisk.

Gust. was shaking his head. "My friend's had plenty of experience on the Atlantic. He's your wheelsman. He's just too much of a shy Norwegian to say so."

I let the claim stand, if only to show him what a man could be.

Ya, well I didn't quite sink the damn boat. But was it my fault the pilot didn't speak a word of *norsk*? He never even pointed out the difference between those red and black buoys in the fairway. I had to figure it out myself, and then I got them reversed. Still the pilot had grabbed the wheel from me long before we grazed the shoal. And then tried to blame it on me. It was only a bit of a scrape. A couple of deckhands fell down, maybe.

I don't recall what words the Captain used, only the way his eyes scorched my cheeks. But he jawed the pilot too before he dropped him off in that little boat. As soon as the coast was clear, I tried to paper it over.

"The pilot said *fire, fire* points to starboard."

"He said he feared for his life, you dunderhead."

48

Captain Fryling even barked at the mate who come to take the wheel.

"Tell your friend to get up here to the wheelhouse."

"Christ, Magnus," Gust. said through his teeth. "I thought you said you shipped along the coast. What in? A fish boat?"

I couldn't lie when he knew better.

"My train ticket run out in Buffalo. So what was I supposed to do? Go live in a Lutheran mission house?"

The bulge of his cheeks screwed his eyes shut.

"We could have gone down in the harbour! Then the insurance companies would have had us blacklisted when we got out of jail. My god, Magnus, you don't even know—"

I give him my best grin.

"Ya, sure, make a big fuss because you just been made the wheelsman. Just don't say I never did nothing for you."

"You're kidding! With you for lookoutsman? Christ! Well, try to fake it for now. Then we'll have six hours off to teach you everything I know."

He was so excited up there he looked like a kid at the wheel. But he wasn't the kind to look down on me for one measly mistake. He flashed all the hand signals in advance, and I give them back whenever the mate was looking.

The Captain got together with the mate again as the watch ended. The old bugger come right down in the bow for awhile and peered at me with those eyes like gas lanterns. I repeated the last signs Gust. give me, not knowing what they meant.

"I've decided not to throw you overboard yet," Captain Fryling growled before he left. "I wouldn't have hesitated if you were Italian."

So Gust. coached me at mess, and then in our bunks. By the time we come on our third watch in the middle of the Detroit River, he said, "We might get by."

I was scared that stream of boats coming by in the river might not. There was so many of them scurrying for port, you could almost leap from deck to deck.

"Well," Gust. said that night as we got ready to stand another watch out of the St. Clair River, "how do you think you'll like sailing for a living?"

I pounded my mitts together.

"Who says this is living?"

He grinned as if he could count on me now.

We crossed Lake Huron most of the next day. But by nightfall we were icebound in the Soo River. The slush ice packed in around us, carried by the current, till some said it reached clear to the bottom of the river.

We sat around our bunks, playing cards and waiting. Gust. and the others dug up all the old stories about slush ice they knew, how it sometimes broke free but other times froze over till the farmers come out in cutters to sell meat and supplies. Then a freighter could be in danger of filling with water unless there was coal for steam to drive the pumps.

"We're in luck then, aren't we?" laughed a tall man with just a fringe of curly hair. "Not too many will be carrying cargoes of hard coal screenings."

"Ya sure," Gust. said without a care in the world. "When the other boats want to use our bunkers, and they send wheelbarrows over the ice, who do you think the old man is going to use for coal passers?"

"Not me," I said ruefully. "I'm going to be studying poker. I've got to find out how you buggers win my money all the time."

The talk come round to women. I let the rest tell their hooer house stories. Gust. didn't say anything though he grinned whenever a storyteller looked at him. I waited till all were done, then told bit by bit how a shipmate of mine had been fleeced so bad by Martin and Ottilee. When I got to the part where the shipmate went flouncing across the street in his housecoat, his shins bristling like rose bushes, the boys laughed till one of them begun to choke. The rest thumped his back like he was no more than a mattress. I didn't crack a smile. All of a sudden I knew what was meant by *poker face*. Here I'd been content, like Gust., to play just the cards I was given.

In the late afternoon me and Gust. tramped into town with the others. The sky blushed like a bride behind the woods. While the other guys went for cigarettes, me and him strolled around, looking at the sights.

"You should come and stay with me in Duluth," he said after awhile. "We could make do if we did a little ice-fishing. I know some girls up at the Normal School, we could have a good time."

"You're a good friend, Gust.," I said truthfully. "That's why I wouldn't want to meet your sister."

He turned red as an overheated stove.

"You don't think that I—?" then broke off, licking his ruby lips. "Ya. Well, to tell the truth, I'd like you to help me land this girl I know. She won't go out with me alone. I figured with you there to take care of her friend—"

He looked away from me for a minute into a store window. It was a shoemaker's shop, boots with their tongues hanging out. Then he glanced back.

"I have to tell you something. Your girl is spoken for. Georgie— Georgina Halliday is her real name— is going to marry a rich guy who's away at college. There's no future there for you, just some good times through the winter."

I was curious. "Halliday doesn't sound like a Norwegian name."

"Her mother is," Gust. said in a rush. "They've been in this country two generations. They're not as stuck to Norwegians as we are."

I figured there must be nothing wrong with her looks if a rich guy wanted to marry her.

"Does this Georgie speak any Norwegian?"

"Ya," Gust. give me a sidelong look. "But it's not real Norwegian. You might think us kind of funny."

"If she understands half of what I say," I give Gust. a sly smile, "it's not me you need to worry about."

He laughed as if he was relieved.

"You'll really come and stay with me? I have the upper storey of an old house. You won't even have to pay any rent."

I hadn't forgot that pimp in Brooklyn, Martin Ness. But I remembered the way Gust. had bloomed trying to explain my discharge book to Captain Fryling. He couldn't lie to save his soul. So I must stand by him if he needed me.

The next day the ice in the river went out in a sudden thaw. Great floes banged into us, bunching around the bow. We could feel it grinding the length of the hull. We made it into the locks by evening, then steamed out through the ice-choked river. I kept seeing great icebergs loom up in my sleep, so damn tired from the lookout. I knew when I woke up what had put the lamp in Captain Fryling's eyes. But there were no more storms like the one Gust. had lived

51

through. Lake Superior let us pass with hardly a cuff of its paw. I was never one to stare off into space, not even in a bow. So how was I to see my storms lay further ahead?

Duluth was a rock stairway going nowhere from the lake, stone bluffs that couldn't pass for hills back home. Still one glance out Gust.'s gable window was enough to give me the feeling of home. We overlooked a row of houses on Superior Street, then a street below where we could see just rooftops, then ice and sky like water.

"There's not much else to show," Gust. apologized like a real Norwegian. "I hope you don't mind sharing a bed."

"I hope it's no trouble," I started to say.

But Gust. was onto something else.

"What do you think? Can we afford to take those girls out tonight?"

I fingered the new greenbacks in my pocket. Amerika might really be a land of opportunity for more than the likes of Martin Ness.

"You're sure there's enough room in that bed?" I said to see him blush.

The Normal School was higher up the bluff. We scrambled like a pair of mountain goats, not bothering to go round by the road.

There was a sort of waiting room in the front of the girls' residence hall.

"Bertine Moen," Gust. said to the girl at the desk. He said something in English too, I thought it might be about Georgie. But I could see he was very awkward.

The girl wasn't gone long. She come back alone.

"She's washing her hair," she said in *norsk*. It must have been to rub it in, he bloomed like such a rose. I got a feeling I was wasting my time here.

He give me an embarrassed look, then spoke more dogged than before.

"Would you ask Georgie Halliday to come down then, please?"

"Do you have a list?" the girl spoke real sweet. "So I won't wear myself out on the stairs?" But she swept out of the room before Gust. could say anything.

I was surprised when she come back with another girl, just a glimpse of her at first on the stairs. Then I seen a shapely skirt, nice small breasts, finally a head of shiny black hair curled round like vines at the temples. Her eyes sparkled so bright it made you happy just to have her look at you. She walked right up to Gust. and give him her hand, then turned to me too, letting my look go so deep she laughed and even blushed a little.

I could hear Gust. mumble our names. Then he said more boldly, "We were wondering if you and Birdie would care to come with us to the nickelodeon?"

Her eyes danced from him to me.

"Are you here for Gust.'s sake? Or did you come to ask me out?"

Her voice was merry as her eyes, everything about her so lady-like and dainty.

"I'd have come on my own," I said quickly, "just to be sure Gust. wasn't making you up. His ravings didn't do you justice."

"You're very gallant," she coloured prettily. "But I know who he thinks is pretty."

I would have protested if she'd have allowed it.

"It's very good of you," she said more coolly, "to include me in your fun. I'm nearly married, you know."

I could see she was warning me, but I only laughed.

"I'm the kind, I should warn you, would stand up and protest when the pastor called for objections."

Her touch on my arm was light as her laugh. I could smell her hair like a cloud of beauty around me.

"Should I run up, then," she touched Gust.'s arm too, "and see about Birdie?"

Her voice went up so musically, I felt my insides turn upside down. Gust. only nodded his thanks, too grateful for words.

The moment she was gone, I said real mad, "What's a rich guy doing leaving a girl like her alone?"

Gust. looked at me kind of sober.

"Don't get your hopes up." He muttered so the girl at the desk wouldn't hear. "She's glad enough to marry into money, you can be sure of that."

"Who said anything about marrying her?" I blurted. It made us both snigger like kids. But what I was really thinking was how to put off that wedding awhile.

It was half an hour before Georgie come back, looking so pert and bird-like that my heart give a little hop of its own. We had only just met, and here it seemed like I had known her all my life.

A shorter girl was beside her on the stairs, brown, furry hair framing her twitchy grin. Still it wasn't a real grin when you saw her up close. Her mouth jerked back in a kind of monkey grimace, exposing her molars.

Gust. remembered his manners. But all he could think of for starters was that I come all the way from Norway.

"Oh," Birdie said and looked at the floor.

Georgie smiled.

"Do you gentlemen know we have a curfew?" She pouted a little, as if to dare me.

"The Dean said no later than ten," Bertie interrupted, pulling a signed piece of paper out of her coat pocket.

"Well for heaven's sake," Georgie slipped her hand through my arm, "we had better get started then, hadn't we?"

We went out into the cold. Gust. asked was it alright to walk till we found a hansom? Both girls said they didn't mind. We strolled down the hill in pairs. I let my body brush up slightly against this lovely woman beside me, feeling us both get comfortable. Then I asked the question that had been left hanging.

"Your boyfriend doesn't mind you going out like this?"

"Fiancé," she said firmly. "He's at Yale. We agreed that we would miss too much in college if we couldn't go out with the crowd."

I had heard the English word from poker players who finally got mad at my winnings.

"Why would you want to marry a guy who's in *yale*?"

"Oh," her laughter pulsed like starlight, "oh, you mean *jail*, the English word! Oh no, I'm afraid it's nothing like that. Yale is a great university in the East."

But her laughter was kind, appreciating my mistake.

"I'm sorry," I laughed too. "There's lots of things in Amerika I don't know about."

"No need for apologies," she patted my arm. "You warned me you never quit before a race was over." Her laugh pealed out again like a lovely bell. "You don't waste any time though, do you, in getting rid of your competitors?"

She turned merry eyes on me till I blushed like another Gust. Then she must have thought she had offended me, touching her cheek to the shoulder of my coat. I squeezed her arm tight in the cradle of my arm.

54

At last we hailed a hansom on Superior Street and clopped in style, glad to huddle against the cold. Gust. pointed out our house as we drew near, the upper storey in shadows.

The nickelodeon was new to me, crowds of people willing to stand in line in the cold just to get in. I didn't let on I hadn't a clue what to expect. Gust. said we had about a half hour to wait. The girls didn't seem to mind in the least. They talked about "Little Mary" who was new that year, and all the men they thought were romantic. They made it sound like there were plenty of these, none of them looking a thing like Gust. or me.

The hall turned out to be an old storeroom filled with kitchen chairs.

"Our swanky place in Buffalo," I said to Gust.

"What's that?" the girls both asked.

We acted like it was something not meant for their ears.

We all stamped our feet trying to get warm. A mob of people stood along the walls, just the hundred or so of us with chairs. The lights were dimmed, a good thing for me. Because I nearly dived for the floor when that locomotive come bursting through the wall at us, steam shooting out on all sides! Then another train took its place, rushing across the wall, and I could see it was only moving shadows. Oh, my *norske* ignorance nearly give me away, quite a man of the world I would make with my face on the floor! But no one had ever heard of movie parlours in Norheimsund.

Georgie accidentally brushed my arm. I felt for her hand, then quivered like a kid when she did give it. A pianoplayer thumped and trilled while we watched the trains speed in and out of tunnels. The picture flickered to a halt.

"Now it's the girl with the long curls," Georgie squeezed my hand.

I couldn't believe my eyes when it was Georgie's face on the wall, the same kisscurls at her cheeks, and the same eyes lighting up her surroundings. I must have gasped right out, "It's not you, is it?"

She only laughed and squeezed my fingers tighter.

In a way it was our story. I couldn't read the words after each picture, but I could tell that the girl with the curls didn't want the lover her folks had picked for her to marry. She was always kind and polite to everybody, even to the suitor, but her face just lit up when a young guy come by. He was poor, had only a few horses, where the

55

first guy lived in a great mansion with the girl and her mother. Finally she had to do something about her feelings. So she sneaked out one night to meet the underdog and they went away to live in a little cabin. But outsiders come to take their land and house away. They had to move on till finally the young husband was shot and the girl was left to suffer. I almost cried myself at the end. Georgie took her hand away to blow her nose. I was already half in love with "Mary" and half in love with Georgie, not sure who was who.

We sat afterwards at a soda fountain and tried to hide our red eyes from one another.

"*Jeg fila så baed, jeg ha kaetscha kold,*" Georgie sniffed, then took out her hanky to blow her nose again.

"What kind of *norsk* is that?" I made it sound like my voice cracked just in disbelief.

"Oops," she touched her hands to her lips, then her and Birdie were both lost in gales of laughter.

Gust. was the colour of a beet.

"It's *Norsk-Amerikaner.* We don't all know real *norsk.* So we don't say much in front of real Norwegians so as not to get in *trubbel.*" Then he realized what he had said and yodelled with laughter.

It helped to get over the unhappy ending.

"Tell me more about your boyfriend," I said to Georgie. I felt I could take anything.

"What's to tell?" Birdie answered comically. "He's rich, we're poor."

We all laughed at her heresy.

"You women don't even know what you want," Gust. said sort of rueful.

Birdie flushed with pleasure, then grimaced.

"I just want a cabin," Georgie folded her arms across her breast like the girl in the picture, "to live in with the man I love."

"The man she loves," Birdie warned me with a twitchy grimace, "is John Smith, star tennis player and man about Yale."

It was my turn to laugh.

"What's so funny?" Georgie said quickly. She tilted her head to one side, cheerful but wary.

"John Smith was the name they give me when I got off the boat at Ellis Island."

Gust. got the giggles at the thought. But the girls didn't believe a word of it. I told the whole story then, starting with the Galician couple who were nabbed at the top of the stairs. I made everyone feel the strangeness of being in that swarming hall.

"You see," I said to Georgie, "you can have John Smith in the mansion. Or you can have him in a cabin."

It was to be our joke after that, Cabin John and Mansion John and who was winning at the moment. But she wouldn't let me win even a kiss at the door, though twitchy Birdie give Gust. a light peck. Gust. kicked up his heels more than once on the way home.

"I don't know how to thank you," he didn't seem to notice my silence. "Do you think," he said again when we were climbing the back stairs to our apartment, "that I've really got a chance with her?"

I said it looked good. But if love was blind, Gust. was already a goner.

The next day we went out toward French River to Gust.'s fishing place. It was in a deep cove where the ice was thick. We tramped down from the road and looked his shack over for damage. We spent the rest of the forenoon getting it skidded out over the ice. We sawed a hole for water, pouring buckets around the plate of the shack and icing down snow on the corners. All the time we were working I saw Georgie's face on the rock bluffs, shining like a moving picture, or looming out of the snow at me. It was as if she had got behind my eyes.

In the late afternoon we caught a ride into town with the local fish dray. No psalm of David was going to keep me away from a man's promised wife any more. I had to make her mine.

The next night we went out to a different nickelodeon. Gust. and Birdie headed out first. While we paced along more slowly, Georgie told me about her home in Grand Rapids and her father's big farm along the *røvver*. *The* røvver, she said. It turned out to be the Mississippi which even I knew about. When she was a girl, she said with a little laugh, she had longed to go floating down the *røvver* on a raft and sleep under the stars.

"I used to wish I could be a boy," she sounded wistful. "I thought it was easier for boys to meet people and have new experiences. We girls were always so protected."

I give a tug at her arm, pulling her close to me. "Do you still wish you were a boy?"

57

"Heavens, no!" she give a brilliant laugh and nuzzled my shoulder with her cheek. "You know, though, I had to fight to get away to Normal School. My mother and father are still frightened to let me go teach. They worry about the big brutes of boys in our one-room schools. I might have been at home yet if John hadn't argued with them."

"Is it because he wants you to know more brutes?" I tried to make a bad joke of it.

"Probably he doesn't want to be ashamed of me," she said sadly. She had never been one to sound sorry for herself.

"I like you just the way you are," I put in a word for myself. But she only laughed.

"I've not been *poleit*," she used another word I didn't know, "to go on about myself. I'd like to know more about you and your life at home."

"My father's dead," I said matter-of-factly. "He lost his whole shipping line before he died. My mother and three sisters were crushed by his death. But his debts are what nearly finished them."

"Oh, Magnus," Georgie said with all her warm interest in people, "I'm so sorry. Why didn't you say something sooner? My *trubbels* are nothing, really."

"I didn't want you to think I was asking for sympathy." I give a careful little laugh. "Especially after the picture show we saw the other night."

Her grip on my arm was like a gentle scolding.

"No, really," I looked into her worried eyes, "I didn't want to take advantage."

"But what will your mother do?" her eyes shone with sympathy. "How will you help them from so far away?"

"If what I hear is true," I said slowly, "Amerika is still the place where fortunes get made. I'm going to pay off my mother's debts before I build my little cabin."

She looked at me as if I was a whole head taller than her, not just two inches.

"I think you're heroic," she said softly. Then she reached up and give me a fleeting kiss.

It caught me by surprise, the taste of her mouth lingering so sweet. I caught her in both my arms, kissing her a little too rough. She started back a ways when my tongue found hers, but in a split second I felt it like a touch of eel on my own.

"Georgie," I pleaded. I could hear Gust. and Birdie's footsteps going away down the sidewalk.

"No," she pulled back in confusion. "Please don't try to force me. Magnus, I mustn't."

"You may call me John," I tried to brush it off with our old joke.

But she avoided my eyes, then pulled at my hand to follow the others.

Still the memory of that kiss lingered through a picture I didn't give a fig about. Touch itself was like a sentence half-spoken, waiting for the answer. It was the real reason I would start that silly quarrel later, not as she thought because of her funny dialect.

We were riding in the hansom on the way up to the dormitory. Birdie said it was still early, would we like to see the city from the top of the bluffs?

Georgie answered she must have another sweater then, could we wait till she ran up to her room? But the words come out queer— "*mens jeg rønna upp på romme mitt?*"

The ones I had been waiting for were different.

"You keep mixing me up," I said like a fool. "I wish you'd decide to speak real *norsk* for a change. Get rid of all your funny English words."

"_____," she spoke English to show me.

"*Jeg rønna upp på romme mitt,*" I warbled.

Birdie and Gust. both laughed nervously. Georgie jumped out with hardly a backward look.

"Hold the cab," I said to Gust. over my shoulder.

I caught her before she was halfway to the door.

"You're hurting my arm," she said in a sharp voice, more like a man. "Don't act as if you own me."

"I'm sorry I hurt your feelings," I said gently. "But don't you see I'm jealous of this other side of you? I can't compete with your English. Won't you let a poor Norwegian boy have a fighting chance?"

After the absence of an evening, her mouth found mine. I felt sealed to her with my soul.

So we went on having fun that way for a few weeks yet. Gust. and Birdie were always close at hand to help remind her. But we both felt the rush of time, Christmas drawing closer. We didn't talk about it after she broke the news that John was coming home for the holidays, they would be together in Grand Rapids.

Sometimes I was mad at the whole group of them, sitting in the drug store and talking their funny language as if I wasn't *norske*.

"*De syntes det var harmeli*," Georgie said of some neighbours in Grand Rapids, "*de måtte sitta der i tre år og lusa kråppen*."

"How did they get that many lice on their bodies?" I said in my innocence. "That it took three years to get rid of them?"

Well, you'd think they'd be ashamed to scream that way in a public place, laughing like such fools. Finally, Gust. had to translate it for me: These people felt it was a shame they had to sit there for three years and lose their crops. But when he stammered again and shook with laughter, and then Georgie gasped like I was giving her convulsions, I could only laugh like some guy glad of his lice.

The next day I convinced Gust. that our *trubbel* was we had no place to be alone with them.

"Let's bring them back here," I said.

He looked at me as if I was crazy.

"If Mrs Fedde finds out," his lips pursed crimson, "we could be looking for another place to live."

"It's worth the risk, isn't it?" I said cool as you please. "The girls are both hot to trot. Hell, Gust., it's the last chance I might have to persuade her."

"She's already engaged to be married," he said stupidly.

"And it's marriage I mean to propose to her."

His face was scrubbed with pain.

"I'll do it," he said, licking his lips. "But I doubt it will do any good. You don't know this guy, John Smith. It isn't just that his father owns a string of hardware stores. John is so damn good-looking, he ought to be the one in the movies. Don't forget, Magnus, that Georgie isn't Norwegian. Her father is English, you know. She's more used to American men."

"I can't forget all that," I let out a groan. "But how in hell's name can I forget her? It's like hell, Gust., you don't know."

He only shook his head in sympathy. So I was hopeless, save for the thought of my music. Maybe if I was to buy another fiddle and make it plead for me...?

But the girls surprised us both, no pleading called for when we asked would they like to go some place more private. On the way down from the college, Gust. give me a wet grin. We didn't waste more time, either, on pictures or sodas. We stole up the outside stairs in back of the house, going quick by the windows on each landing.

"That was *isiere* than I thought," I winked at Georgie while Gust. was opening the door.

She rested comfortably against me for answer. But in the glow of a newly lit coal-oil lamp, her eyes sent out tiny darts of light.

"You might learn American yet," she teased me with a soft laugh.

Gust. took Birdie through the sitting room to the window overlooking the harbour. I was shaking like a reed in the wind.

"Come here," I said in a fluting voice.

She never took her eyes off mine, looking amused, excited, happy.

"I'm really crazy about you," I said, "I want to mar—"

Her tongue met mine and took away all words. We kissed as if we could breathe through one another's mouths. My hand rubbed in her skirt, then up into the furrow of her corset.

"Not here," she held me gently away.

I led her aside into the bedroom.

"Don't close it," she said.

"Why not?"

"I'm keeping my promise. I only go out in a group."

I held her with both my hands on her hips, buoyed up by this lie she had to tell herself. When she shuddered, I thought she would go right down on her knees. But her face rose level with mine.

"Touch me again," she murmured. "No, not through the skirt, up here, under the hem."

She hitched her own skirts up in the front, my hand stroking the soft flesh of her thighs. She hissed through her teeth as I pried the rubber aside, then clashed her teeth against mine.

My jaws ached, so tired I wanted to quit, so frenzied it was like my scream at last when her mouth fell away and her whole body went stiff, jerking like a dying animal.

Afterwards she said, "Poor darling. What can I do for you?"

"I only care about you," I drank in the dark, secret odour of her hair. But I knew I had everything to gain by sticking to the high road.

She nestled against me, fingering my shirt buttons.

"I know you do, Magnus. I'm all mixed up, I care about you so much."

I was sure then she was mine, won from some stranger who could only damp her Norwegian spirit, making her a *jaenki* like him. Our kids would be Norwegian too, my soul not lost in this country. But then I remembered Gyda and I thought, Who wants to be Norwegian? Georgie was the reason I left father and mother behind. From now on she was my only homeland.

It was almost a week before I learned what kind of immigrant I was. Georgie and Birdie were taking exams, we only got to see them for a bit on Saturday night.

"At least we'll be finished," Georgie said, "by Thursday afternoon. We'll still have Thursday night together before I go home for the holidays."

I spent the money from my week's haul of fish on a good suit. Even Gust. said I didn't look like a foreigner any more. He didn't look right at me when he spoke. I knew I was a pain in the neck when he'd been so kind to invite me home with him for Christmas. It was a comfort to know I would still be close to her through the holidays. But it drove me crazy to think of her with John Smith.

Birdie stood up as we come into the sitting room Thursday evening. Her lip kept twitching in that terrible grimace.

"Where's Georgie?" I said with a sinking feeling.

"She's got a bad cold," Birdie wouldn't look me in the eye.

"Couldn't she at least come down to see me?"

"Nurse said her fever is too high. She told me to give you this."

It was a lovely photograph of Georgie, her chin cradled in one hand. *To Magnus,* it read. *Love always, Georgie.* Maybe it was the way her eyes still danced off the page that raised my drooping spirits.

"I'll have to give her my present in the morning," I said sadly. I was such a dope I never thought to get her something.

Gust. looked at Birdie as if to warn her. I tried to pretend I didn't notice, while all the time truth was waiting round the corner. It threw a pall over us, we weren't the same at all without Georgie.

"We can still go to the pictures," Gust. said lamely. "Unless you'd like to tag along with the Christmas carollers."

"I think I'll just go home. You don't want me to tag along with you."

"Oh no," they both said at once, then faltered.

"You shouldn't sit home alone so close to Christmas," Birdie said with a grimace. "Besides," she give a hollow laugh, "we wouldn't know how to act without you."

"Ya," I said heavily, though I couldn't have stood to be alone. "Well, it's pretty good of you, I'll say."

The picture show turned out to be cold comfort. It wasn't only because my kisscurl girl had such a small part. A gang of thugs was trying to bust into her house where she was alone with her mother and sister. The mother telephoned frantic to get her husband. As I watched them ruffians at the door, something clicked inside. Gust. tried to grab me as soon as I jumped up. But Birdie held him back in his chair.

"Magnus," he hollered after me, "Magnus, don't be a fool!"

I tore up the hill like all hell was after me, feeling hell open wider inside me. I knew I was too late even as I tiptoed up the back stairs, hearing nothing any more, not even the whisper of my feet, but only her remembered cry, wild beyond longing, aching with beauty, till remembering merged with the sound through my bedroom door, her voice thrilling higher and higher, a cry without bottom, where I wanted to fall forever.

I took one peep through the keyhole and seen a lily white ass like a lung gasping for breath. A dainty pair of heels fluttered like a pounding vein in my temple. Then something went click again and the picture got far away, like something seen on a wall. I followed my feet out to the kitchen, waiting to see what my hands would do. They raked through a clutter of drawers till I felt my palm slice across a blade. Butcher knife. Blood spurted across the counter top, then down over the flowered linoleum.

I crept into the bedroom where they were heedless of me and waited for my bloody hands to tell me what to do. It was the same old story, someone always there before me. The knife paused over the jiggling, butting sack. Blood foamed down my fingers, the blade a part of my hand. And then my mind turned clear and cold as the night outside the window.

"Don't mind me," I said in a deadly quiet voice, "just don't make a sound."

There was a snort like pigs stampeding for the trough, then a real confusion of buttocks, faces, legs.

"Magnus!" Georgie let out a gasp, cut short by the sight of my bloodied knife.

63

"_____," said John Smith, looking like a dog with his knob caught in a knothole.

"Tell him to lie down on his back," I waved the knife like a brush over a painting.

"Magnus," Georgie looked so white and frightened, "what will you—"

The knife outlined her face. She spoke a rush of English words and Mansion John got right down on his back. His mouth was pasted shut with dried spit. His yellow hair spilled into his eyes like dung.

"Tell him you were with me here before," I said with hate as sweet as love.

She cringed.

"Go on, tell him."

Her eyes begged me not to betray her. Not betray *her!*

The words were said with lowered eyes and such grace that for a moment I could almost love her again. John Smith's eyes told me she had spoke the truth.

"*Vaer så god,*" I said real *poleit.* "Now lie down right on top."

She bit her lip, making up her mind whether to scream.

"If I get my turn," I said evenly, "I won't have to cut you."

She bowed her head and knelt, a nun at her altar.

"Not that way," I said with a surge of grim joy. "Get his thing right up inside you."

"But how—" she looked behind like a rider from a horse.

"Lean right down," I said at a gallop. "Now spread a little farther. Like that." I could see his probe stuck up beneath that other red ring. His face was lost in a shower of black hair.

"*Vaer så god,*" I said looking down on what I had made.

But it was tighter going in there than Lokksund at Malkenes. Once she jerked as if to pull away. Mansion John only laid like a dead man underneath.

"Do that again," I said in spurts, "and I'll nick your pretty face."

She slumped and only whimpered a little as the gates give way. And Cabin John come right along, bringing up the rear.

Soon I could even look ahead to where the naked couple groped for any rag to cover them. And as I mounted to heights beyond all height, I knew that here I was really first for once.

Hilda

My fate was sealed that third midnight I came creeping past Papa's door, back toward my bedroom, and his voice surprised me in the dark like the touch of love. Hilda, he said so sadly, do you know where you are going? Then I stood in his doorway, feeling so unclean I wished I could have a bath that moment. I wanted to go light a fire to heat the reservoir and scrub those scales of fluid off my belly, scour myself clean inside and out. But I said instead, He loves me Papa, he won't let any harm come to me.

He's no good Hilda, said the voice in despair in darkness, there's talk of other women.

I had never heard him sound so hopeless, not even when he wept and called himself my sad Papa. How could I help but believe him? Still I couldn't help myself, Magnus had awakened something deep in my nature, and I would risk the future for sake of our quick harmony.

Papa, I said, please forgive me for being your sad daughter.

There was nothing more to be said, he saw I was as helpless from love as he was from drink. I went to my bed and lay there. Through the wall I could feel him thinking of all that was lost, Mama from consumption and the brick house that burned. He didn't want me to be lost as well to a faithless lover. But Magnus, when I left him, was snoring in the hayloft. So why wasn't my way the right way to make him forget other women?

I awoke to hoarse cries outside my bedroom window, hardly the dawn crimsoning my curtains like that, and still a great voice baying away till it suddenly growled, Get avay from here, go on, you've made your trouble, you vant more? Those words at least came clear, though the source of light did not, swirling like fire, the hoarse cry rose again, Fire! And then I came to my senses, my bedroom floor like a plunge into water, but only the pitcher on the dresser to quench the roaring breath of flames. Yet those flames, when I drew back the curtains, were as silent as northern lights, as if fed by the snow itself nearly a foot from the wall. For a moment breathing was a musical rest, till the hurt was transposed beyond all harm, and I might have stood stonestill and listened had not Magnus bellowed, Hilda, break the goddamn vindow! There he was dancing head and shoulders above the fire, till I saw what was wrong, the flames went curling behind the house!

Oh the harm was real alright, my loved ones such heavy sleepers! I ran through the parlour where light danced in the glass of Bonneted Maidens, then over the keys of my grand piano as if to mock my maiden's fancies.

Papa, I cried banging on his coal-black door, Peder we're ringed by fire!

In the half-dark of Papa's room a figure was dancing into trousers, rose-tinted shades dancing with him on the ceiling. Peder turned back from the window, his eyes kindling in fear. Don't be afraid, I said calmly, Magnus is going to take us out through my window.

A terrific crash sounded in my bedroom. I ran back to see a fence post, wrapped in flame, combing the sash. Little shards of glass hit the floor. Magnus, I cried as the wall of fire wavered, now gave way to a man's face and shoulders vaulting the sill. Tiny curls of flame lit in his hair. Then he was safe inside with me. Wait, I said quietly, I'll get my coat and boots.

But he ran out to the parlour before me. Gunnar, he yelled, you'll catch the *blankety* door on fire, come out my vindow.

Then he was back with my winter things, sweeping me up, my face tucked under his chin. I felt him stagger under his load, fumbling to get a foot over the sill, shifting us out, before a wave of heat washed over and we surfaced in cold that still couldn't touch us. In the darks of his eyes I watched the flames part, my loved ones coming through, and still I stared as into a crystal ball. Had he betrayed me already?

Get scoop shovels from the veat bin, Papa hollered. Magnus dumped me like a sack of hot potatoes on his way to our monster granary. My bare feet burned with chilblains. Then I spied my boots dropped in the snow and stood like a shivering blue heron to pull them on. Papa had his parka off, blanketing the flames. I felt wind under my nightgown as I flapped my best winter coat.

If he was with that woman, I said aloud to the shapes of flame, he sent her away, she won't be back. But the flame leaned away, returned with my upraised coat. Blue flames danced out of sight around the corner. For the first time I thought of my music and all my art work there inside. Oh, I cried to the dark above, he wouldn't willingly have hurt me!

Magnus was back, Peder with shovels, one for each of us to bank the fire. Foursquare we scooped drifts now where the flames burned soundlessly, by magic it seemed, without touching the wall. I turned a scoop of snow over to a sudden poof of flame, damping it in one motion in the depths of the snowbank. But I couldn't damp the shock which the smell of kerosene gave me. It underlay all and refused to go away, even while the fire fluttered under a steady whump of snow. I met Magnus at the corner of the building, our shovels ringing together in a metal flurry, snuffing out the last flicker.

Whoever would do such a thing? I said to him, gasping for breath over my scoop shovel. The hint of corruption sickened me.

Your friend Dagny, he said cool as you please, she vas alvays after me.

Well what fools one can be, I stretched this to mean he wanted to be faithful. Ha well he spoke the truth at least about Dagny, her Dad pulled up stakes next morning and left his debts behind him. Then it was only me left to face the music.

Nammen there isn't any music now, only some blame fiction on TV. Many's the time I could sleep in my chair with TV going full blast, but never before during *Spotlight on Talent.* I guess tonight there is no help for me, I am awakened to all those deep things left in my nature. *Uff da* even my feet are asleep, stabbed by tiny needles as they hit the floor. Oh my balance is no good, have to catch myself on the piano bench! Then I notice I am rummaging under old sheet music inside the bench. *Nei,* not here.

In the spare bedroom my hope chest is piled high with old boxes, even pails ha in case a fire breaks out again after fifty years. I tumble all down onto bed in my anticipation, the brass-bound lid giving out a musty breath. There it is! My stiff claws click over records as I rush out to the front room.

I pull the turntable down like a Murphy bed and lay my treasure on it. Even my hand recalls which band it is, though my poor old heart is not to be outdone, catching at once on sustained notes of the oboe. Finally it is released into a sigh of strings, falling a fifth each time. And then Birgit Nilsson's voice is simply yearning with the violins, a farmgirl like me though she has learned to live apart in song, her voice now thrilling *O Siegfried! Herrlicher!* soaring nearly off the scale before touching to earth again. Then as always my eyes betray me *treasure of the world* and I sit with great tears sprouting like corn.

As soon the surging of strings is stilled, rest, resuming in the major key. I reach for Kleenex to blow a great trumpet blast ha. I feel so broken and yet my heart is quieted. Strange how nothing helps more than to cry sometimes. I remember how I wept when Papa confessed his mistake about Magnus. Hilda, he said, you don't vant to lose him, marry the man who vill go through fire for you. He thought my tears were just for joy.

But I had known I was a goner the moment Magnus played at that barn dance, not music like this but simply thy-will-be-done of the fiddle, so joyful and quick I couldn't care what came after. Once the music stopped I tried to collect my wits. Mr Hedin, my teacher at Grand Forks Conservatory, would peer at me over his spectacles and ask was I another silly girl not cut out for a concert career?

Then the band struck up like swallows leaving a wire together. Even the farm boy who held me stepped more lightly in front of the timid ones seated on bales of hay. But I had eyes only for that stranger who played with never a care in the world. Why did I seem to know him? And how was it I felt his every wish in unison with mine?

Dagny Guttormson danced by to ask over her partner's shoulder, Did I know him, was he the reason I went sneaking off to Grand Forks? Then the wheat-haired boy who had asked me to dance bloomed like a prairie lily.

The music stopped, time for me to stop too, as I was starting to wear my heart in my shoes. Thank you for the lovely polka, I said to the tow-headed boy, feeling sorry for him. He looked at me, eyes as blue as flax flowers and said, Ya, you're not so swell you don't know what goes on in a barn.

Whose turn now to blush but mine? I didn't know where to look, wished the floor could open and swallow me. But even as I turned away in confusion, I was met by my fiddler come to hear all. Oh, my shame still roasts, spreading over breasts neck face, so hot.

Nammen not all that's hot, have to make a dash for Parliament ha, but these blame water pills make it so I can't hold it sometimes. Oh if Magnus knew he would laugh right out loud, not just the twinkle in his eye that night saying he enjoyed my predicament. Here, get the door open, I'm still not used to back-in as Mr Peterson the plumber called it, no room to turn around. I have to spy my face like a beet in a hairnet before I settle beneath the mirror. What a thing it is to get old and lose so many of your faculties. Still it's better to be alone where no one can see your shame. I couldn't stand to be carted off to that new Sunset Home by the highway as one is never alone, always someone to point the finger ha, so no rest for the wicked. I sleep most afternoons but there it's all younger people, quite a few from Lacjardin and just oodles of ladies from Nisooskan, so it does seem the men die younger.

Then it smites me, have to catch my breath. Oh I will be a widow soon, I should have been used to it before now, but how could I be when he forsook his family for the fleshpots of this world? Christine wrote how glad he was his girls had come to be with him, now he wasn't so scared to go any more. It was a great weight off my chest too when they said there was no one else. As if I were still a young girl desperate to get him back. Well my goodness, you'd think I would be resigned by now. Could I be more widowed than I have been for half my life? Could not, and yet his death threatens to undo the knot tied that night by fate.

Nammen my bloomers are soaked right through, good silk too. I'm no better, really, than Magnus, as the girls wrote what a hodge-podge they found in his cabin. He has no control left to his bowel, the mess tracked everywhere. Even after they scrubbed, the cancer smell lingered in the wood.

Ha my place might have to be fumigated too when Christine gets home, my eyes so bad now I don't see the dirt. I'm sure I couldn't have survived this long without my dear girls. I would have been taken to the asylum the day he left were they not here to pick me up. Their lives were ruined too as a family but they stuck to me through all. It's only right they should get to see him now, as I expect he'd hate to have me witness him in such straits. Poor Magnus, it was his own doing as he left me for a real tropical woman who made money that way and fleeced him of his miner's cheques. What fools one can be. I never got a dollar from him when he was still home. I scrubbed our school every month to get four dollars and divided all with my girls to get stockings as one never went without stockings those days.

Uff da no help from my elastic stockings now to get off Parliament. Poor old feet are so carbuncled it's a wonder I could ever dance at all. I try to shift weight to left foot so it won't cramp so bad. He would never recognize me though, my face as sapped as a baked apple. Even my same old curls are dusted with icing sugar, where he would be looking for such dark, thick hair of the wild woman from Borneo. What did he ever see in me, I wonder? not the prettiest girl at a barn dance, already a hint of double chin, my cheeks as fat as a gopher's. I must have weighed 140 then, same as him, though his bones and feet were more delicate. Even now I can't hide such elephant legs, and my hands creep into my lap the moment visitors drop in. If only I wasn't always compared to girls with feet he said were dainty!

Ffffah I'm staring at the mirror like a lovestruck girl and here I am clutching wet bloomers still. They should be rinsed in warm water and laid out to dry. There, I think the stain all came out, they should dry decently now. Oh but I was never that kind of girl, no matter what the wheat-haired boy blurted for Magnus to hear. It was his music I was given to, the reason he took a whole month to court me.

Nammen have I gone and left the TV blaring with the record player on? Oh, thank heaven that's all it is, my goofy brain for once might be good for something. I know I wouldn't miss such music for

70

the world, really like old times to hear a Scandihoovian from North Dakota play an accordion like that. Magnus could have met him too, just starting out, and gotten famous for more than dirt. But I have to wonder sometimes if he doesn't blame me. His band was really going somewhere, touring all through the Dakotas, when he turned back that Christmas to be with me.

Lawrence Welk smiles, Don't they just give you goose bumps folks?

Poor Papa, what an addition he had to face when Magnus begged me to stay home from Grand Forks Conservatory. I didn't know what to do as Mr Hedin said I might have a real concert career before me. Vell Hilda, Magnus said all pickled with hurt, I give up my band to come after you, and they've lost their blame bookings.

But Papa looked at me almost as broken as he did at Mama before she died. Hilda, don't throw your life away, his eyes said quietly. *Now's the Time to Fall in Love,* says Mr Welk, a real beautiful little tune. Okay Jack and Mary Lou, take it away.

Oh yes, we danced to that tune and look what we made of it. I'll never know why he felt he had to ruin my life.

I sit in my big chair and tears roll down my cheeks, getting stuck in the wrinkles. I was crying my eyes out that day too in the coulee, with my face hidden in the pussy willows. Open water tugged at ice along the river. I could almost be hopeful in such mild air, save for my little bastard, not meant to bear the worst with me. Through a blur of tears I glimpsed Magnus step out of a thicket on the far bank.

Hey Hilda, he grinned over the water, you up the stump or something? You look like hell with those red eyes.

I must have burst right out howling.

Vell I be damned, I heard the soft explosion of his breath.

I didn't dare look up. The dark water went sliding between us.

You sure the kid's mine, Hilda? he said after a time. Then I felt my anger flare like a neverending blaze.

If it's not, then I'm the second coming of the Virgin Mary.

Ya, he said all too slowly, I hear she spent some time in a barn too.

Well I couldn't help myself, I wasn't going to live with some blame words blurted thoughtlessly.

Magnus, if you believe what Dagny hounded that poor farm boy to say, you're not good enough for me, I don't care if you did go through fire for me.

71

It was the biggest speech of my life, maybe I should have run for Congress.

He grinned in real surprise.

Vell Hilda, ven should ve book the church?

I'm three months late already. You suppose I want to parade myself in a church? Anyway, what makes you sure you want to marry me?

Hell, ve got six months at least, time to take off a crop yet. Your Dad said to stay and farm vith him. Ve yust started seeding a little early.

But how was I to know Sigfrid would be born a month too soon, and still almost six pounds? All I could think of during the birth was my mother's death, and how my poor little infant would perish with me, like the baby lain in Mama's coffin.

Mrs Johnny Johnson, our neighbour lady, was there, nothing to do for sudden labour pains but to give me a wooden spoon to bite. Soon it just hurt and hurt, I didn't even care if I lived or died, just let this pain stop. But after nine hours, when the little shoulders finally pushed through, there was a whole new world of pain to consider. Was it even alive, were all its limbs straight? There was a slap, a sharp little yell. She's fine, Mrs Johnny Johnson said, a dandy baby girl. I thought of Magnus, how little he knew of girls, and decided to live, if only for her sake. But again Magnus surprised me, bumbling into my room like the bee in clover. I think there were real tears in his eyes, the man made over for once in the woman's image.

Ya Mother, he said almost shyly, she's a beauty, she reminds me of my own dear mother. Could we call her Sigfrid?

He had called me Mother, so truly satisfying! Before, I had been determined to name her after my own dead mother. But the note of appeal in his voice was so touching, I couldn't refuse him. Only the name Sigfrid confused me.

Isn't that a boy's name?

Nei, in Norvay you hear it alvays as a girl's name.

Well I wasn't a true *norske* like him, maybe I had got the story wrong. I was one great cauldron of confusion ha but I didn't want to cook my daughter's goose.

The next week threshers came to our farm, late September but so awful hot my kitchen was bearable only at breakfast. Sigfrid fed at my breast four a.m. while I fired the stove, fried potatoes, steak and eggs for the gang of men bedded down in our barn. Papa and Magnus were out already feeding the horses, the engineer gone to the fields to oil his machine. I hurried poor little Sigfrid through her paces, shy to be seen before men. She was already asleep when they came in, and I was nicely buttoned up to wait on table. But farm boys are not the kind to be cowed by nursing mothers. While I poured coffee, a string-haired man spoke to a whiskered one.

Alf, you should have dreamed what I did last night.

I did, Alf licked his red lips and glanced at me, I dreamt of great hills like camel humps.

String Hair wet his mouth and stole a look at me.

Would you say the hills are bigger here or down at Langdon?

The only hills anywhere near Walhalla were the walls of the Pembina River valley. Then I noticed all eyes on my bosom. With my face like the rose, I tried to think of a more delicate subject. Through the window I spied our fine big rooster, Rhode Island Red.

Oh look at the cock, I said.

The men all rushed to the window, even Papa and Peder. I felt so relieved until I heard a great clap of laughter. I looked again, where my scapegoat was treading a dowdy hen. She hadn't even been in the picture when I spoke! Oh my misfortune meant to follow me up and down the barnyard! Magnus, when he sat down, looked at me as if to say, Make a fool of me, vill you?

Now it was his turn to divert all eyes, strutting out a story. But I watched how men listened and all admired him. Well thank goodness I was spared the spotlight.

Ve never had to sit, he said, and vatch some animals back home in Norvay. The animals there vatched us. You see, it's the girls who tend the cattle all summer long vay up in the mountains. They sleep alone in their *seters,* you bet.

And he winked at Alf who had forgot all about his camel humps.

But come Saturday night, do you suppose you could find a single boy at home along the fjord? Not us, he grinned. Ve vas all caught up into heaven. Ya, it vas still vun hell of a climb with a fiddle in your hand, maybe a sqveezebox strapped to your chest. The girls had got all dressed up, too, in their vedding colours, red and black, and cheered at first sight of us boys coming above the tree line. Then you bet it vas more than cowbells ringing as ve played our instruments the rest of the vay. Even the calves had to kick up their heels. And as soon as the sun vent down, Magnus said lightly, every girl vent back in the grass with her boy and did vat come natural.

I half believed him myself, there was such an ache in his voice.

How come, one boy said after a wistful silence, we're so backward here in North Dakota? When will our girls ever go for free love?

My first thought was at least I wasn't a dirty joke to them any more, Magnus so particular about his own position. But oh how he left me open to every kind of doubt! How many Norwegian girls had even been left with their babies? Were there weddingbells beforehand, perhaps, to make mine criminal? Oh, wasn't he the smooth one to have the story both ways? In public I was a ball and chain to him, keeping him from the good old days, while in private I was the hussy scheming how safest to stain his bed.

The men scraped back from our table, hungry for more picturesque stories where all could laugh and roll in the dirt. I started to clean up scraps from the plates, then changed my mind and lit the stove. I had plenty of sour cream and cheese, I would cook a whole pot of *rømmegrøt* for my breakfast.

That night in bed I must have sounded too eager to ask, Were the girls really like that up in the mountains?

Ha, Magnus's breath stirred the hair along my neck, they really vent for that vun, hey? I had to yump to beat your sporting cock, Hilda.

Then I was sure he didn't understand me.

You could have said something sooner, couldn't you? Why did you leave me to fend for myself? I didn't know that rooster was going to disgrace me.

Silence lay like a sword between us.

Magnus, you don't think I'd point to a thing like that? To a group of sex-starved men? Whatever do you take me for?

Ya, vell I counted up to nine, Hilda, same as the rest.

But he couldn't have meant it like it sounded.

You know you were bloody from my first time, Magnus Sigurdsen. That's your daughter sleeping in the bassinet, your baby *Sigfrid*.

Ya sure, my eight-month daughter, too bad I vas a little late for the Christmas goose.

How could I have slapped my husband? Oh it was done before I knew it! I had never hit or been hit before in my life. Surely he must kill me now or leave me.

Magnus let out a great shout, laughter which took my breath away.

Ha ha Hilda, I can yust picture your face, same as that *blankety* hen ha ha ha.

Then I was so confused I didn't know whether to laugh or cry.

The day my second girl was born, there was good reason for tears. Christine came too soon again, no one home with me but Sigfrid, only two years old, and a baby arriving so fast there wasn't time to run for Mrs Johnny Johnson. I couldn't even boil water, Magnus's cruel joke about my cooking made by circumstance. For my own water was broken, contractions now coming three minutes apart. Oh, I should have paid more attention to these signs of low backache all the forenoon.

I pleaded with Sigfrid to go play in the parlour. But the gasp of pain which took me by surprise held her riveted, nothing I could do under the sheet but make a tent of my knees. Afterwards, I lay with the baby on my bosom, and Sigfrid and I looked in wonder upon this new girl meant to share our fate. Poor baby, she seemed so sad and knowing, yet determined not to cry. I told her her name was Christine, after my dear mother. I could only hope I would bear my sorrow as bravely as her.

Sigfrid took her nap tuckered out in bed with us while Christine took my nipple. Then when the baby was burped, I left both to sleep and got up, sore and pained, to kindle a fire. When at last the water boiled, I dipped our old butcher knife by its wooden handle, counting sixty. Poor little baby shuddered as the blade trimmed her cord to a stump, freeing the afterbirth. But soon she was swaddled up in sleep, and I set about to tidy up after us.

I was in bed for the night when my men got home in the early hours. Papa had long since taken Magnus to his bosom, Magnus returning a kindness by dragging my brother Peder on their drunken exploits. As I shuffled out of our bedroom, Papa tried to hide the blame bottle he was pouring from. Then his eyes took in my condition, seemed to sober instantly.

I'll go for a doctor, he said almost by apology.

We'll live, I said softly, mother and both her daughters.

Magnus was dealing cards on the table and onto the floor. Peder cursed him, cursed his cards, cursed Mr Loken the banker. Magnus laughed, not a care in the world. He didn't see me yet.

Papa, I said very deliberately, her name is Christine. You should see her, she has Mama's beauty and her stoic graces.

Papa looked so guilty for an instant I thought he would bolt. Then he shook his head to and fro.

My dear, oh my dear, I left her so awful alone.

Papa, it's all right, I'm sure of that now. Believe me, we are sometimes best left alone.

Gunnar, Magnus looked up, where's that drink you—

His eyes, too bright already, lit on me. We looked at each other without heat, without anything for a moment but recognition.

So you really can do it all vithout me, eh Hilda? he said at last with a grin.

I gave a toss of black mane over my shoulder and went back to our bedroom. Christine was still bound tightly in her blanket. I listened to her soft breathing, so free of any fretting. Finally I slept in spite of such a fracas in the kitchen.

Magnus was snoring beside me when I woke up at the baby's quiet stirring. A light shone under our door, Papa most likely sitting mournful by the table. But when I dragged myself out with my dear little bundle, it was Peder brooding in a great fury of smoke. A dozen cigarettes had been stubbed in the tobacco can lid.

Phoo, I can't feed her in all this combustion.

Sorry, he spoke almost automatically, stubbing the sooty thing. He glanced with sudden attention at the baby taking my breast, then eyes flew away.

How did you ever manage by yourself? his voice was hushed.

I shook my head. I didn't know what to say.

You won't disturb her by talking, I offered. She's so patient, just like our Mama was.

Then the sight of his white face hurt me worse than anything that night.

Peder, what's wrong? It isn't like you to sit alone.

His hands fumbled with more tobacco and paper, fingers quite as long as a concert violinist's. He had grown so tall, yet so thin, I was smitten with a fear of consumption.

Peder, you're not sick, are you?

Christ no, just so damn sick of myself.

Have you—taken to gambling with the rest?

What else?

Christine released her hold on my nipple. I covered myself, putting her up on my shoulder for a burp. The chill I had taken wasn't from the drafty window.

Has Magnus—are you the only one losing, Peder?

Hell no, Papa's worse than me. At least Magnus wins back Papa's share. Otherwise that damn Loken would own us outright.

The smoke was creeping our way. I got up to spare baby's tiny nostrils.

Here, I didn't notice, I'll put the damn thing out.

Peder, what if you went away somewhere to work? This drinking is no good for you. I never dreamed I would be fretting over you the same way I do over Papa.

He gave me such a funny look.

You don't think that's what I've been doing too, Hilda?

He stood up then and left me to reckon his meaning. I was so blame tired I couldn't think, I dare not think. The sun would be out on the morrow and there'd be hope.

I must have gone on hoping a couple of years past any reasonable hope. Peder left that spring, like so many before him, to homestead in Canada. I wrote every month to Nisooskan, Saskatchewan, such a strange name for a place, as I thought then. He answered one or two letters. I didn't know how to tell him about the frantic drinking, worse all the time. I told instead about the girls, said Papa and Magnus were same as usual. But I knew Papa would drink himself to death if I let him.

Such scenes, after I couldn't put them into words, haunted me till I had to do something to get them out of my system. I risked oil paints until the night Magnus tried to behead poor Papa. Then it wasn't any use. But I know that image will go with me to the grave, a true painting in it somewhere, Papa lain down on the chopping block like a lamb, eyes closed so tight, only his face serene and quiet. He and Magnus had been out this time for days, both so drunk that neither would stoop to unhitch the bays from the cutter. The great beasts stamped and stamped, their harness bells jangling, until I knew I could never step between their traces. So I had to listen to poor brutes, Papa and Magnus drinking in our kitchen, the bottle slamming again and again onto the wooden table till I feared the coaloil lantern must tip over, trapping my little girls in a last house fire.

Afterwards Magnus blamed me for the argument about horses, said I was always one to come between friends. I only raised my voice for the sake of that poor team, catching their deaths in thirty below. If I wasn't so mindful of right, I might have asked Papa to humble himself, I know he would have done it for me. But he wouldn't take orders from Magnus and they argued something terrific, each telling the other to do it, pouring oil on the flames with long bobbing swallows straight from the bottle. Then Magnus wiped his mouth with the back of his hand, snatching up Papa by the scruff of the neck.

Ya, he says, you're so chicken to go out in the cold by yourself, vell I go vith you.

In his shirtsleeves he carted him right out the door, Papa's limbs flopping like Sigfrid's rag doll. Who wouldn't have thought the worst? I watched in terror where Magnus combed the woodpile between horns of snow, and then where Papa knelt to rest his cheek as on a pillow. When Magnus raised the axe I couldn't look, couldn't even think, my feet racing the other way to Johnny Johnson's yard.

Behind me I heard a horrible clap of laughter. And I turned to see my father and husband clapping backs on their way to the kitchen. The poor horses were still standing in their tracks. At least it was easier now to brave the stamping beasts than to face such inhuman laughter. I squeezed past the horses' rumps with eyes shut tight, hardly caring what happened to me, though dumb animals showed more pity than men, waiting perfectly still while I loosed them, trace chains and all. Then I led them clopping behind me to the barndoor at the bottom of the coulee.

Hours later, when I came back from the blessed quiet of the stable, Magnus and Papa were still drinking and cavorting like cronies.

Ha Hilda, Magnus says to me his eyes gleaming with drink, you should have seen this old banty so mad vaiting for the axe to fall. He tvists his head clear around like this and he blinks up at me. And ven he sees how I hesitate, you know vat he says? *Drep meg. Ikke vent for lenge. Jeg blir død og borte.*

78

Kill me. Don't wait so long. I shall be dead and gone.

Oh yes, a true painting there somewhere, only how to paint it? I really believe Papa was given up in that instant to his fate. Thank goodness it wasn't an outcome to satisfy Magnus, not content unless he could mock at fate. But I could never figure out myself how to paint men laughing themselves to death.

Karen knew what I meant this afternoon as she had to spite her mother to marry Wayne. I suppose Mrs Babiuk wanted Karen to marry a Ukrainian boy and stay on the same side of town as them. But a fat lot of good that does, doesn't it? Didn't I marry a *norske* like myself? And then such a fuss when Wayne wouldn't put up with strong drink at the reception to spare his Mom's feelings. Karen had planned for a real oldtime Ukrainian wedding, like the ones I played at as a girl, and her Mom took such a sliver when they had to cancel the Hall. But all is long forgotten, Karen such a dear to write me every week when Wayne is too busy. How it gladdens my old heart to think she would come and see me today in my great need. Still I was pretty scared when she phoned to ask could her Mom come with her? We don't mix as Mrs Babiuk sticks to Ukranian ladies, like so many others on their side of town. I hardly dared to let her see my shack and me as I am ha, as she might carry tales to SkiTown.

But it turned out Mrs Babiuk is a dandy Easter egg painter, and she looked at all my old plank paintings, horsedrawn cutters and the like, and plaster-of-paris mallards. She even put in an order for some, though my hands are too cramped by arthritis to make them any more. I gave her the ones she seemed to like most, so I can't regret the bare spots on my wall. We even got into my old photo albums after awhile. It seems I can't help myself today, I must try to go back to those old times. Mrs Babiuk was glad, though, to be reminded of our funny hairstyles. Then she noticed our old car.

Did you marry that man, she said sort of oddly, because he drove a nice car like that?

No, I said in surprise, that was my Papa's car. I don't know, though. Magnus might have intended to marry just the car.

She didn't stumble to my little joke.

My Metro was the first one with a car to come by our poolroom in Lacjardin. But I still had to work so hard when we were first married.

You had it worse than me, I said kindly. Papa sent me away to study music when I was a girl. I went to the Conservatory in Grand Forks. But I got my share of overtime after I was married. Then I had great stacks of white shirts and coloureds to do for people so I could feed my girls. I guess that's how I got ulcers, and eating too much pork ha till doctors said no pork at all in my diet. Though I do cheat once in awhile.

You got stomach troubles too? she asked brightly.

Sometimes I eat so much, I grinned, that I have to gulp Maalox for ulcer and gas. Then I have to wait for pop goes the weasel ha!

The way her broad nostrils got so narrow, I held my breath for fear I'd slipped. Oh, I hadn't meant to demonstrate!

Oy boże, she said brightly, you mean you fart!

I sniffed. Then I was sure the coast was clear.

Nammen, such an old windbag I am to sit and chew the fat! Here I've gone and forgot to put out the eats! Karen, why didn't you remind me?

I know I was no good after they came, but I might as well croak if I can't make my visitors a little lunch. And Karen is like a real grand-daughter, she understands how I feel. Was it ever something to have a chance to use my rusty old jaws, my only comfort now that my own flesh and blood are gone to be reconciled to their father.

While Karen helped me butter the *lefse*, I asked, Do you think Wayne will go out to meet his granddad?

I don't know. She seemed to be watching something out the kitchen window. I can't say any more what he plans to do.

But I know Christine would be so happy to have her son join her now. I know too that my girls never really understood why their father would leave them. Maybe he wants to take some of the blame at least. But more than likely he's told them just his side of the story, which is only fair. He will mock me, saying it was all meant to be.

I could never get used to that awful mockery, maybe because I never understood it. I remember that one night when Papa and Magnus were celebrating spring, great flakes of snow clinging like moths to the windowpane after weeks of warm weather. Magnus raised his glass to Papa, peering with red eyes at him.

To spring, he laughed.

To Banker Loken, Papa said gingerly.

Their glasses clanked so hard, I thought they broke. But their hooting only made them set their tumblers down before the drink spilled out. Papa began to beat the table with his fist, as if more was in him than might ever be laughed out. Magnus joined in his thumping, both heads bent as in a real musical duet.

Papa! Magnus! I protested, you'll wake the girls!

I was furious at both anyway for waking us at all hours. I was sick of competing with rum for new dresses for my girls.

Can't either of you give a thought to a decent sort of home life?

Magnus fell howling off his chair, pounding his fists on the floor. Papa grinned sheepishly up at me, still in a stupor.

Papa, do you want your granddaughters to see you like this? Don't you feel ashamed what they will think?

He peeped down at Magnus beneath the table.

It don't matter now, Hilda, it's all over vith me.

A delicate hand reached over the table's edge from below, fumbling at the glass of rum. The glass was suddenly tipped and poured thoroughly. Magnus stood up with the wet streaming out of his hair.

Ya, it's all over me too.

Papa's solemn expression gave way to childish glee, such hooting catcalls. Still all was forced. I feared to face the worst.

Drink, Papa raised his glass to take me in too, for tomorrow ve die.

Magnus winked into his empty glass.

Or go to blazes in Canada, vere the best rum comes from.

It made me sick to see both grown men giggle like girls.

To Peder in Canada, Papa said ruefully, to hell vith Loken.

Ha, said Magnus looking out of the window, it looks like hell yust froze over.

Then it came to me like a lightning bolt, my day of reckoning. Oh I'd denied for so long what Peder couldn't say to me.

Magnus, you gambled away our farm, didn't you?

Ha you see, he snorted so contemptuous of me, you see Gunnar Braaten? Vat did I tell you? She blames me like I said she vould.

I could have crowned him.

It isn't enough that you sold our best furniture, is it? Maybe you'd like to be rid of us all. Papa, you said he was no good, how could you let him ruin you too?

Papa struggled to stand up.

Blame me Hilda, I'm the vun who ruined you at poker. Blame me for losing my blasted shirt.

Papa, why did you let him entice you away from us? You cared for us more when you were really our sad Papa.

Even as I wailed, he tore at his shirt, buttons flashing in air like filthy vermin.

Blame your drunken Papa, he said over and over, such a drunken Papa, but your sad Papa still. And he up and bolted for the porch, gathering parkas, coats, overalls, all that was hanging on his way out of doors. Won't you do a thing to stop him? I cried at Magnus grinning in the door like the court jester. Then I pursued him myself, fearful he would strip like a Finn and roll in the snow. Papa, I cried when I saw him sprinkling garments with a bottle from the midst of his bundle, Papa wait!

But a burst of flame scattered snowflakes like feathers. Papa skipped back unscathed from his little bonfire, standing like a child now to watch all burn. I stopped still as Lot's wife, waiting till the end with him. Then we turned our backs on the little pile of ash and walked from house to tenement.

Magnus stood blocking the doorway.

Ve had enough of fire around here, he said. Come on Gunnar, I help you to bed.

It was his tenderness that thawed the ice in me. Oh I cried like the Missouri while they bumped around in the next room. And then I wept like I did at Mama's funeral.

The bed sagged beside me where I lay facedown. Fingers combed in the tangles of my hair. I couldn't face him yet, couldn't bear to have him lie to me.

Ve put our names on a bill of sale, Hilda. It's all gone, house, horses, everything. There's no place left for free land but up in Canada.

I wouldn't let him touch me. But at least he told the truth. The next day some men came to take Papa's horses away.

That night Magnus took me by the hand.

Come on outside, he said softly.

The full moon shone through the window as we tiptoed past Papa's gaping door. The parlour, without its sofa and lace and my grand piano, hurt like a missing tooth. Magnus helped me on with my old rag of a coat. Then we were outside on a field of trampled snow. I looked back for our two sets of footsteps, but all was mingled into one.

Magnus took my hand and we skidded downhill where the loft door opened from the hillside.

Where are you taking me? my voice caught with surprise.

You don't have to be so quiet, Hilda, them blame horses are gone.

Poor Papa had followed as far as the gate, watching the road long after his twelve strapping Percherons had passed from sight.

Ya Hilda, you remember how scared you used to be that the horses vould hear?

The barn was silent beneath us. Cold seemed to seep through the floorboards littered with wisps of hay.

Magnus pulled me down with him on a low pile of hay.

Magnus, I can't, it's the wrong time.

The hay was beginning to give our heat back to us. Magnus unbuttoned his fine new coat, pulling it over us. Then he was shrugging out of his trousers, thinking only of himself as usual, I would be the one to face the consequences.

Magnus, we can't afford to make another baby.

He fumbled in his coat pocket, tore a corner of paper, and raised the coat like a tent.

I vent to a drugstore today, he shuddered with the rush of air over his belly.

There were snapping and crackling sounds, taking forever to unroll. My embarrassment, great as ever, kept my face turned into the hay. But my body gave all away as soon as he touched me. I wanted to be one with him like before, to match myself to his strong rhythms, climb mountains up and down with him, always with him.

The next morning we pulled out at dawn, Papa driving the Ford like an ice box, even with bedding packed tight as cotton batten round the girls and me in back.

Mama, Sigfrid said, will Canada be warm?

Nammen the album flops on the floor as I heave up to see what car is leaving. But I only catch the taillights before they wink out at the T in our short street. So Bakkes must have had some company, I didn't hear a thing. Oh, and I've missed *Lawrence Welk* completely, TV blaring away to beat sixty. I press the button, banishing my last company. But I am not fit for man or beast tonight. It's such a nuisance to hope that others will think of me. Maybe Magnus would remember me at death's door. Are the girls with him at the hospital, I wonder? Would he maybe find it in his heart to speak kindly of me before his eternal passing on?

Why should he, when already he looked so sick that day we got to Peder's place? He gave it one glance, then ever after it was my fault we had come to this godforsaken place. We couldn't even get to the homestead by car, but had to walk in from Finn Ottoson's on a trail through April-sodden bush. I carried Christine, Peder holding Sigfrid by the hand, not shy at all to see her uncle after two long years. Magnus stumped along, paler by the minute at the sight of such a solid wall of bush.

Next year, Peder was saying, I'll have proved up my quarter and we can finish clearing our homesteads together. Do you know, the first year my breaking went sixty bushels to the acre? That's wheat mind you. Can you beat that? Not much like the old Dakota days.

We stepped around another bog oozing out of the trail. Magnus's cheeks were close to the same shade now as the poplar poles hemming us in. Only Papa looked about him with an air of one returning home. He breathed deeply, little sighs of contentment, though he carried two goodsized grips. I guessed his boyhood in Gjovik, Norway was coming back to him.

How do you get your eqvipment through all this bush? Magnus spoke abruptly.

Ha I worked my way in here with a damned swede axe, excuse me ladies, a grand swede axe. It's a backbreaking job but you get used to it. I tell you, there's nothing to take your crop away here but frost, no other natural enemies. Remember the year in Dakota the army worms came? How they were three inches thick on the ground, and when they worked they sounded like squashing cornflakes? Well, we're free of all that now. If we beat the frost we can buy new land too, three dollars an acre for *add pre-emptions.* I tell you, they were wrong back in the States, this is the real land of opportunity.

My arms ached, I couldn't carry little Christine any farther.

Magnus, will you take your daughter for a ways?

He gave me such a funny look, I thought he'd seen something behind me in the trees. But he did pick her up gently, setting her high on his shoulders while I gathered my stack of sheets and quilts closer to my breast.

I want a ride too, Sigfrid said shyly to her uncle. He swept her up proudly, then stalked off like a lord among his potholes, almost running with the spring run-off. I looked ahead at a sky washed blue, as much as could be seen through these bare bones of bush. There was nothing to do but tramp on, holding our heads and linens above water ha, while mud and mulch clung to our shoes.

When we came at last into a stump-filled clearing, it was my turn to feel bleached. Peder's house was nothing but a sapling shack, how could we ever crowd beneath that lean-to roof? Peder read my mind, his eyes quick and bright as a bird's, with head cocked to one side.

I know it's not what you're used to, but we'll get all that back and more, you'll see.

But Magnus, when we came inside the cabin, wouldn't even sit down. He paced the plank floor as if something needed to be measured. I saw the floor required a good scrubbing, have to wait till morning when the girls and I were alone. Right now, I needed help to get the stove going for the first pot of coffee in our new home. Peder anticipated me in all. He finished his work by reaching into the little curtained cabinet and bringing forth two great sheets of flatbread.

Peder, wherever did you learn to do *norske* baking?

He blushed red as a firewagon, then blurted all at once.

I had some help from Ketil Torgersen's daughter. We're getting married as soon as we're a little better situated.

Oh Peder, we must be in your way! How awful for you to be stuck with a bunch like us.

I looked at Magnus, wearing a trail in the floor, oblivious to all but his disappointment.

I couldn't hold my tongue any more when he was still sulking at bedtime. Here we lay privileged on Peder's wedding bed with our girls bundled on the floor behind a curtain. Papa and Peder had only a makeshift den at the far end of the room. Magnus, though, was going to have none of it, where before he never seemed to let me alone.

You're acting like a great big baby, I whispered to his back. You haven't shown one sign of gratitude to Peder for all he's done for us.

Ha!

He turned so sharply that the quilt fanned my cheek. Then I could feel him on his elbow, hissing above me.

I'm not grateful to you, you mean. If you hadn't sent him up here, ve'd still be on our farm in North Dakota.

I was always to blame, no use even to argue.

But when Peder's girl came the next night to supper, Magnus had completely changed his tune. He got all spruced up in his wedding suit while I was still fretting over the meagre pork chops that would never go round. Oh I should have held my nose and cooked that venison Peder cured himself. Though what a dandy impression she'd get of me, serving wild meat with my hair run amok! Well, six pork chops would have to do to let her know we were once civilized. I would split mine between the girls and take more of scalloped tomatoes and crackers.

The door opened, Loretta breezed in like the song of a meadowlark.

You must be Hilda, Peder says you're a wonderful musician. We sure need you to get some barn dances going. Oh say, what lovely dresses for your girls! I know, your name is Sigfrid. And I'll bet you're Christine. Can you come and give me a hug? Oh such pretty babies, give Loretta a smooch.

They went to her too where she knelt with outstretched arms. Peder looked at me and I let my eyes speak my pleasure in his choice.

Magnus showed his pleasure more directly.

How about a big hug for your new brother-in-law? Ya, there's a girl, Peder knew vat he vas doing coming up to this country.

Loretta looked at me helplessly over his shoulder, smiling her innocence while he grappled her. The moment he let go his hold, she darted under his arm to embrace me.

Oh we're going to be such good friends, I've wanted to confide in you since Peder told me all about you. Did you bring your oils and canvases? Peder says you'd rather paint than eat.

I liked her tremendously.

My poor style is nothing to look at. But look at you! Such a beautiful girl! Oh, Loretta, I'm so glad Peder chose you.

Vith a name like Torgersen, Magnus interrupted, you must be Norwegian too. Vere you ever in Norvay? No, that's too bad.

And he went on talking so brightly about nothing that I didn't have the heart to put a stop to his showing off.

Peder got up to find some tobacco lids for ashtrays while Papa tamped his pipe full. I was surprised when Loretta took a cigarette from Peder's box, but really flabbergasted when Magnus took one too! He never smoked in front of me, not even when he was drunk. He always said the fumes made him want to choke. There was nothing I could even do to spare poor girls from the furnace, having to stay put by the stove. Sigfrid was so pleased, though, to sit on Peder's knee, and Christine with Loretta, that I surrendered them gladly.

While I took the scalloped tomatoes out of the blackened oven, I prayed that Magnus would be decent for once and spare us his version of *seters*. The tomatoes were still too runny, so I crumbled more crackers into the stew and hoped for the best. When I could pay him any mind again, he was telling lies about his days as a sailor. I watched his hand trace the air almost like a paint brush.

Ya, you can bet ve vas scared pushing into that hole, ve never knew if more pygmies lurked in the dark. But it vas empty of all save a hoard of treasure. Oh, there vere goblets of gold and yewelry galore, you should have seen the stuff. And a chest full of coins. Ya, you girls remember Daddy's little sea chest? Vell that's the vun, it vas crock full of treasure.

Magnus looked so intent, he wouldn't see the mocking smile on Peder's lips, or Loretta's eyebrow arched at me.

Daddy, Sigfrid piped up, what did you do with all the money?

I took it, Magnus's smile was like a stone thrown into water, and give it to the Sailors' and Pygmies' Mission.

The grownups roared through all the smoke, leaving me trapped on my side of the room. Oh, I did fret too much over what people might think! Magnus wasn't even giving Loretta the glad eye, only trying to make himself believe this was a land of opportunity.

After that I tried not to worry so much. But when Papa and Peder would go to the field every day, and Magnus would be off to beat bushes of a different sort, it was hard to take things so lightly. While the ants sweated, the grasshopper fiddled. And what would become of the grasshopper's children once winter came? We couldn't go on taking Peder's hospitality that long, not even if I went to the woods myself with an axe.

87

But in less than a week Magnus came home in the forenoon, catching me unawares.

Pack up the kids, Mother, I found a place of our own.

My first traitorous thoughts surprised me, lurking how long in some dark part of my mind?

Where would you get money unless you stole it?

Who said a vord about money? I yust got crop shares vith old Arne Hagen, he's decided he's had enough. He said he's bushed, he's getting out today.

Then I felt so bad to have slandered him, I couldn't think straight.

We can't go away and leave Peder hanging. Don't we owe him a hand until his breaking is done?

Ya, he couldn't be bothered to joke with the likes of me, you're always crying how I don't do my share around here. Vell, I found a farm of my own to run. There's horses in the barn vaiting to be fed. So are you coming or staying?

There was nothing to do but go over trails we had trudged nine days before, this time riding with our few belongings on the jolting hayrack. The girls held to the front wall at first, watching woods and dried-up gullies come by us. Then Sigfrid seemed to feel something more was called for, she dashed from front to back while the wagon bounced beneath her. Christine tried to follow, only her tiny feet lost their nerve. She crept shyly back beside me and clung to my skirt, feeling the bonerattle through her clicking teeth.

The thud of axes came to us above the crunch of iron-rimmed wheels. Then I saw a treetop lean before it stooped from sight. Magnus sawed at the reins.

Papa kept looking at the ground all the time Magnus trumpeted his good fortune. Peder looked hurt at first, surveying his acre of stumps. A ray of doubt dawned slowly in his eye. Then his face took on new shape before my eyes, mean and uncertain, like something caged, not a lovely sight to behold. I hoped I hadn't looked like that when Magnus first broke the news. After his piece was said, I at least tried to remember my manners.

We'll be able to help you out now, Peder. We were really in your bride's way before. We just can't thank you enough for all your sacrifices. Papa, you're welcome to come and live with us any time you like.

Ya, Peder's lips quivered, well don't bother to thank me. You should damn well save your thanks for Arne Hagen. Say, if you ever hear of another deal like that one, let me know, eh? I could use a damn sight of luck myself.

I couldn't let my mind dwell on such feelings, so much there to hurt me. I had to turn my thoughts entirely to our new dwelling, a real tarpaper shack as it turned out.

Well, I said after we went inside and my first speechlessness was ended, I guess it's no wonder Arne Hagen pulled up stakes.

Ha, Magnus seemed as genuinely shocked as me, you can alvays tell a bachelor's farm a mile avay, hey? He builds his best buildings for his animals. Vell Hilda, if the vind vistles too loud between the boards, ve can spend our nights in the barn. This one is tight as a ship, too. Vait till you see.

His words made me hope he had some makings of a farmer after all. No other man would take a place at sight of the barn alone, with never a thought for the house.

You go see to your horses, I said, I'll try to shovel out our stall.

Magnus strode out, such a big grin on his face, I could almost feel light-hearted again. Mr Hagen had surely left in a hurry, though. Flies swarmed like magpies over the loaf on the table. An old butter knife was stuck in the jar of marmalade. I almost gagged, pulling the knife from the dough, to see maggots like tiny kernels of wheat.

It took a week to sweep and scrub that bachelor's *seter*. But I could take comfort from the way Magnus worked, day and night, to put in his crop of wheat. We took hot meals right to the field, and jars of scalding coffee to keep him going. We would wait at the corner for the four-horse team to plod near, the girls so excited because Daddy was coming. Magnus squatted in the shade of his team, sucking the coffee through his teeth.

Ya, he smacked his lips, ven I finish this forty acres, ve should have an oldtime barn dance.

He got up and went to look behind the iron seat of his seeder.

Vere's my snuff? he said quizzically, did I lose it in the blasted field?

No Daddy, Sigfrid said from the far side of the seeder, it's not lost. We planted it right here. When it comes up, you'll have all the snuff you want.

The black look on his face brought me between him and my girls. Then his look was gone like a cloud passed in front of the sun.

Ha ha ha Hilda, did you hear that? The girls are going to grow my snoose. Oh hahaha. Ve'll have a crop that folks vill pay to see, let alone to chew. Oh this is a land of opportunity, Peder vas right.

But there was little opportunity in sight the day we went to Nisooskan to get our shipment from the box car. We crossed the railroad tracks and Magnus flicked the horses into a trot along the main street. He held the reins up so, really putting on the dog, until ladies on the boardwalks stared and then glanced away.

We pulled up in clouds of gritty glory in the CPR yard, my face surely as maroon as the wide-roofed station. Magnus hitched his team to a ring, then stepped off onto the oily platform. He stalked along, unconcerned by all the staring eyes. The dropped stitch in their gossip, still too quiet for us to hear, was gathered up.

It took two men to lay the iron plate from the car door onto the rickety wagon. The station agent kept it like a shield between them. He was a stout man, his great florid face burning as if in shame to be seen with us.

Why are all those people staring at us like that? I whispered to Magnus inside the door of the box car.

Don't vorry about them, he said careless as you please. Everyvun in this country hates to see a guy get ahead.

I looked back toward the platform where they sat like a crowd witnessing some kind of performance. I don't know what on earth got into me. But in my dusty cotton print, I curtsied like a great actress. Magnus winked, nothing more. And the way my heart lifted, I knew what a thing it was to scoff at gravity. Oh, it gave me a little glow just to think I could be like him! When he drove the team out of town like a Roman charioteer, all eyes turned toward us as we cantered past, but no lips hailed us. We went bumping down long avenues of silence. I was never so glad to leave a place. Peder would not have done us dirt, would he?

I made up my mind on the way home to confront him.

Let me off, I said to Magnus at the gate. I'm going to let Loretta know you've hauled all of Papa's things home with us.

Don't bother, he said with a shrug, as if he didn't want to be caught in a good deed.

I want them to see, I said over my shoulder, that spite is best answered with kindness.

We had to walk three miles north to the Cross Lake district. Poor Sigfrid, I almost pulled her off the ground. And I was clutching little Christine like a *Katzenjammer* mother.

There was no new bush cleared along the last few rods of trail. Nor was any woodchopper or farmer to be seen. Then the very sight of Peder's yard made me break into a run. The house wasn't lived in any more. What told me that? The curtains, I realized, were taken from the windows.

We rushed in without knocking. Loretta was kneeling at the little curtained pantry, packing dishes into a cardboard box. She turned her head with a word of greeting on her lips, cut short by her guilty start.

Loretta, I burst out, what are you doing? Why are you taking my brother and father away from me?

She rose, struggling to get back on more equal footing.

We were going to drop in to say goodbye, at least.

Why on earth would you clear out with your crop already in?

Peder's sold the farm Hilda, she said gently. We're moving to Saskatoon. Your Papa has taken a homestead on the south shore of Lacjardin Lake. We were going to let you know before we left, believe me. I could never leave like a thief in the—

Her disconcerted look told all. Suddenly I couldn't bear her self-righteous little face, so in keeping with the whole town.

I know what Peder thinks, you don't have to try to spare me. Well, you tell him if he wasn't so blame jealous he could see Magnus working his heart out too, we're not ones to take something for nothing. Peder just can't stand to see Magnus get ahead of him.

Loretta was dumfounded. I knew she couldn't answer me now.

Mama, Sigfrid tugged at my hand, why should you be mad at Uncle Peder?

Hilda, Loretta's voice was like a firm hand holding my shoulder, there's something you better know for your own good. Peder asked me not to breathe a word, but you're bound to hear it from someone who doesn't mean you any good. Magnus took that land from Arne Hagen, Hilda. It's what everyone is saying.

I remembered my box car curtsey, such a hussy I no longer knew myself.

91

Here, Loretta said, trying to steady me, and then I felt myself guided to a chair.

And you'll swallow such tripe? I said desperately. You'll turn tail and run because of a few chatterboxes? You're just like all the other sheep in this country!

I'd ask you to leave, she said coldly, if I didn't feel so sorry for your little girls.

Don't go to any trouble on my account. Not when you're so busy feeling sorry for yourself.

And I marched them out the door as quick as we'd come.

As soon as we got home, I gave Sigfrid a package of flower seeds to plant a toy garden. But I had to force myself to go out to the hayrack.

You didn't tell me, I said to the stooping back, that I was taking a bow for your latest crime.

So Loretta told you, did she?

You think it's funny, do you, to cheat a man out of his homestead? You want to come along at the tail end, when all the work is done, and just enjoy yourself?

Ya sure. His face, turned toward me now, could hardly contain such a big grin. You bet I like to come along at the tail end! Oh hahaha what a horse's ass you are, Hilda.

Ffffah you can't open your mouth without some dirt coming out. Always trying to make a mystery out of your filth. How did you do it this time? Did you steal Arne Hagen's land in another card game?

Don't be so dumb, voman, you're missing the yoke! I got our farm by staring up a horse's ass. Oh ya, a real vun, black as a lump of coal. Vat do you think of that? Didn't they tell you about Arne Hagen up there on his five-gallon pail? Yust a humpin' 'er for all he vas vorth? Ya, and ven I said, Vould you like me to back her out of the stall there, Arne? he got so scared he fell off his mount.

I didn't know what to think.

Mock all you like, I said with my head held high. I suppose you think I don't know horse manure when I see it!

Oh my yes, he always said *I* was such a pain in the rear, and now the cancer has eaten from his bowel into his rectum. How I wish I could be there, though, all four of us together one last time. But I expect he would not have me, better to sit home and stew in my own juices and

92

not bring him further misery. Still I have been in spirit with my girls uphill and down to that hospital, walking or even riding in taxis as it was two miles from their Dad's apartment, and I have suffered with them the best I could imagine. Though of course I cannot imagine what Magnus looks like any more, not even a photograph left behind to give me a hint.

My eyes light on the water-colour of Pickerel Lake above the piano. Of course my picturesque scenes always led to such terrible scenes at home, you'd think I would have given up such girlish fancies. Still I remember how excited I was trying to catch those fantastic tones of blue, the cobalt lake mirroring the beautiful azure from a hillside of flax, and all reflected again in the sapphire depths of sky. Each tone on my canvas began to alter the shade of the next until I noticed that the real sky had darkened. Great thunderclouds were crossing the face of the sun, and here I was so absorbed by my masterpiece, my cheap water-colours would have to turn waterproof, and quick!

I got up my easel and palette board under one arm, gripping the picture frame like a stick of driftwood, and scurried off before great blasts of wind. The trees tossed their heads like so many gossip mongers ha. There goes queer Mrs Sigurdson, she *paints* you know, her husband is the blackmail artist, such a talented family.

When a car klaxoned right behind me, I nearly went up a tree. But it slowed coming by and I recognized Matt Gudbrandsen, our former neighbour from Cross Lake district. Tilda Olsen and Winnie Knutsen who sometimes came for coffee said he was the finest fiddler they had ever heard.

Say, Matt said soberly, if you don't get in you'll be drenched. Come on, Mrs Sigurdson, I'll give you a lift.

I opened the door with my painting in one hand and paint-tubes bulging from my apron, so much paint on my arms, I must have made quite the picture myself. There wasn't time to hide my handiwork as the rain slashed at my back and legs. Then I tried in vain to close the door over my easel.

Here, let me put those things in back. Been out painting, have you?

Then he whistled softly.

I've never seen Pickerel Lake look so real, not even when I was looking at it. Would you care to sell me that painting? I know my wife would be glad to have real art work in the house.

93

I was so startled to think decent people would pay money for my poor efforts that I shook my head.

Oh come now, I'm not so hard up I can't afford to put some beauty on my walls, same as a rich man. How much? Ten dollars? Twenty? Fifty, maybe?

He made me so nervous, I blurted ten just to be done with the subject. But as soon as the words were out I wondered, Could I have gotten fifty?

Say, Matt said suddenly, isn't this wind a mare's tail?

The thunder seemed to roll inside my head. I darted a glance at him, expecting to see his face twisted in mockery. But he stared up the road with worried eyes. Oh it had only been his thoughtless expression! Still I felt so uncomfortable I didn't know which way to turn. It was almost a relief when we got stuck in the mud. I insisted I would push, though the clay was so greasy my shoes slipped like the wheels. Now the car inched up the slight rise of ground, lightning playing like a spotlight around us. Mud spurted over me, wetting my legs, dress, face. Then Matt reached the top and stopped. I got back in the car, my appearance matched to my repute.

Look at you, Matt exclaimed, I've ruined your dress. What can I do to make it up to you?

You gave me just what I needed, I said quietly. He thought I meant the painting, but who was I to parade around with decent people? I must remain in the shadows, not able to bear this bright light of day. Oh I would never stray so far again, not on my own.

We passed the school, too early for the girls to come home. Maybe the storm would pass by then.

Please, I said at our half-mile corner, I'll walk from the gate.

I didn't want Magnus to see tire tracks coming into our yard.

Wait, Matt sounded almost hurt, I thought you said I could buy that painting.

You're very kind, Mr Gudbrandsen. I have to paint for myself, you really mustn't take any notice of me.

And I fled up our lane, not hearing whether the car started or not, regretting only that I couldn't repay such kindness. I was thinking too what a fool I was, ten dollars was so much more than I got for sweeping the school and even scrubbing it once a month. But I couldn't turn back and seize the opportunity.

The house was silent as the tomb when I let myself in. In the four years since Peder left, we had added on a room here, there a room, a great maze of logs to hide our shameful secret. I headed straight for the crawl space in the girls' room where I hid my paintings from Magnus's scornful eye. I was well past our bedroom door when the image of a man lying in bed, arms crossed over his chest and smoking a pipe, caught up to me. I must have gasped, startled by his presence as much as by my own red-handedness. He was out the door swift and haughty as a cat.

Vell, so vat have you been up to today? Painting some more, hey? Let's see vat you done this time.

Only Pickerel Lake, it's nothing, really.

I set it down in the hall quite casually, as if to leave it.

Ya, Pickerel Lake, that's down by Matt Gudbrandsen's new qvarter, isn't it?

His voice was perfectly level, only something foul lurked in his eyes.

He did me a favour, if that's what you mean. He gave me a ride because of the rain.

Ya, I can see by your dress vat he give you all right.

Nothing in his foul moods of late prepared me for this, it couldn't be real. I had to step out of the scene, so wrong anyway, and look at what was needed to save it. There I stood in my proper shape, lumps of mud still clinging to my lumpen flesh.

You've found a little hussy somewhere, is that it? And you want to shift the blame onto me?

Ya, he said so aggrieved you'd have thought he really believed it, you're showing me the vay, that's for sure.

Then he changed the subject so fast I was sure I'd hit a nerve.

You better keep Knutsen's hound out of our yard after this. The next time he comes sniffing, I'll blow his damn brains out.

And he clapped his pipe in his mouth, jetting smoke out his nose.

Just listen to yourself, jealous of a poor creature who knows how to love. You'd envy even a dog, wouldn't you, because both your daughters love him.

You let that hound touch them, his tone made me shiver, and I svear to God I'll kill you both.

What on earth are you talking about?

Ya, his sneer turned loathsome, I see it isn't only Arne Hagen on

95

this farm who got a taste for horse's ass. Now the animals ride humans.

He stalked out of the house, leaving me speechless. I was horrified to think what he might do next. Oh, I must be hitched to a mad man!

I'm sure I was relieved when he failed to come home for bed or board that night. But I started to worry when he'd been gone five days. Maybe he'd deserted us, without a penny more to live on. Or else his demon had made an end of him, leaving his corpse to be picked at by crows in the bush.

But I might have known the magpie would come home to foul his own nest. He breezed in with his cronies late one evening, a big grin on his face, asking where was supper?

Where have you been? I ignored his command.

Making our living, he winked at Alf Anderson's brown face. I've took so much from these buggers, now they say I got to feed them.

But nobody touched the ham and scrambled eggs I fried up. All were intent on the poker game. The frantic drinking scared me most, making me think of our last days in North Dakota.

Helmer Kettleson sucked his pipe more often than his rum, his eyes grave and watchful. Even I could tell that he was winning. Magnus played as crazy as he'd begun to talk, bidding, raising, bidding again till Oscar Benjaminson chattered like a squirrel, He's got two little ones, I can tell! I'm going to call if none of you will! And Alf Anderson laughed so loud when Oscar raked in Magnus's pot, I was scared the girls would wake. I always wondered why they called it *poker faced* since they seemed to be able to read it where I couldn't. He only grinned when he made out his IOU's, though they were spread like feed oats around the table.

I had to do justice to my feelings somehow. But the only way I knew was to try to paint the scene from memory in the front room. I was frightened when I could remember every face but Magnus, so awful to think I might really know strangers better than my own husband! I stole into the kitchen now and again, trying to glimpse the man behind the mask of the monster. After awhile it was no use, I hid all away and went to bed in despair.

But who could forget the morning he found my interpretation, snooping away in my crawlspace for whatever reason? He brought it in where I was punching dough on the table.

Ven did you do this cartoon? he said shortly.

I acted as if I didn't give two hoots what he thought.

Oh, one day when I was tired of picking pincherries, I guess.

Ya, vell you should stick to making yams and yellies and looking after your family.

He went to the cupboard above the washstand. The next thing I knew he was slashing my work with his strop razor.

Magnus! I gasped as if the knife cut me, Magnus, stop it! Stop it!

But he went on with his work, not merely slashing the canvas but trimming the faces out carefully, beheading each one as neatly as he would have done to Papa. It was no use even to wipe the dough from my hands.

You've gambled away the farm again, haven't you?

You better keep your blame voman's mouth shut, I'm doing this so my friends don't find out vat a hooer you are. Painting your lovers' portraits right under my nose!

He held my ruined canvas to his face like a mask, peering with one sharp eye through the blank of Oscar Benjaminson's face.

Yust be glad, he said with a terrific gentleness, I don't do the same to your face.

I guess I might have known, the day I found his own defaced image, where things were leading. I opened my photograph album and there were the girls and I beside Papa's car, Magnus with one foot up on the running board. His face was black as any coalminer's, blotted by tiny crosshatches.

It was only a matter of time till Alf Anderson was sent, so drunk he could hardly walk, to fumble in my bed. And after the first time, I dare not even shriek for fear all must come to my bedroom again, Magnus holding a lamp so the men could guffaw and snicker, the girls rubbing their eyes at sight of some stranger in bed with me. Oh no, I would sit awake all night after this, in case my rapist blundered in, to hit him where it hurt. I would at least make him hesitate to do Magnus's bidding.

The girls were gone to stay with Papa by Lacjardin Lake when Magnus stopped pretending, even to himself, any more. The door to my bedroom whisked open, winking the light. But there were no footsteps creeping near, I had to listen with all my wits to catch even the sound of breathing there beside the door. Was it outside as well? I knew all was too strangely quiet for poker players in the kitchen. Too late I heard a stockinged foot beside the bed, no one to hear my appeal any more, decency departed with the girls as sure as sense from drunkards. Still I was able to edge off the far side of the bed. As

97

Alf approached, I felt for a chair. All I could think was, this time they are going to let it happen, this time I will be finished!

He made a sudden lunge for my mound of pillow, I swung at his shadow. The splinter of wood on bone tingled clear to my elbows! He made a muffled sound and lay still. My god, I thought, I've killed him! Oh dear God, I couldn't have killed him!

Alf, I cried grasping at his head, Alf, are you alright?

My fingers brushed his hair, so sticky and wet above his forehead. He lay absolutely still.

Oh Alf, I moaned, Alf, speak to me!

I was cradling his head as best I could when the bedroom door opened, Magnus with a lamp. But it wasn't Magnus, it was Alf and Oscar, then Helmer too! Magnus lay bleeding in my lap. His eyes flicked open. To this day I swear he winked before he got up from the dead.

You see vat I mean, he said unmindful of his blood and gore, she vould have done it for you Alf, she yust vanted me to think she put up a struggle. You guys are my vitness, this voman is a hooer. She vas sleeping vith all kinds of men ven I met her, I didn't know no better. I took her at her vord it vas my daughter. My daughter born to me eight months from my first piece of tail! You guys are my vitness, those kids are none of mine.

It was the dead of winter, school finally closed till spring with roads impassable for all but poker players. Magnus had been gone a week this time, half of it in a howling blizzard. The girls and I huddled with frost sprouting inside our log walls, though safe from the brunt of the storm. Still the wind might swoop down our chimney, when the fire burned low, and snuff out the last tiny flame. I would wake in the dark, feeling something was wrong, frost clinging to my lashes, and rise shivering from my burrow. Two or three times a night I would have to go into the kitchen and kindle the stove, then check on the girls sound asleep with their heads far under the comforter.

After a week I couldn't bear it any more, had to get out to town where other flesh and blood than my own could see me, even stare to its heart's content as I passed. I bundled up both girls with three scarves apiece round their parka hoods, and tied one of Magnus's cloth caps over my ears. Anyone would have guessed I was going to see Dr McKittrick the dentist ha. But first we had to shovel our way through yesterday's tunnel to the barn. The hens' water was a block of ice again in the pail, we had to bring boiling water to thaw it while we gathered our morning eggs. Only twenty-two today, that meant forty-six were not laying, we would be six dozen short. My customers could complain all they wanted, I couldn't give a darn at 3¢ a dozen.

We packed the newly washed eggs into a second crate and loaded both on the sleigh. The drifts from the storm were already hard-packed by the wind, creaking far down the road in front of our feet. Now and again a foot broke through and we would flounder to the groin in powder. But through it all, our sleigh tossed like a good little ship in a painted storm.

We made our rounds down the south face of the hill into Ski-Town where business was best, even before Easter. I was four days early, Mrs Gullickson told me sort of nervously.

Nammen, I said, here I blamed my hens for not laying in such cold. Sometimes I guess it's my brains that are scrambled.

You poor dear, it's too cold to be out. You come any time you like.

Four men with brooms came out of the curling rink. The one with a red face grinned as we tramped by. I thought for a moment he would offer me the use of his broom.

We pulled our sleigh around the spruce trees to Mrs Cherwyk's back door. Her husband was gone for the winter too, to help support her with earnings from a sawmill near Hudson Bay Junction.

Cardboard had taken the place of glass in the crooked storm door. I rapped with a mitt, then bare knuckles. The inside door inched open with a crunch of frost. Mrs Cherwyk stood in her pink housecoat and slippers, lips falling loose, eyes opening wide in the rush of steam. I was about to speak when I saw Magnus bolt up from the kitchen table and out to a back bedroom. By instinct I tried to shield the girls, too late as Christine looked up at me, then touched her face to my old coat.

Here, I thrust two liners of eggs at a face as pink now as that housecoat, you might as well take these too.

Then I beat a retreat before she could drag all out in front of my girls. Neither one said a word but stuck like lint to me all the way home. Both took it for granted we would not go to the stores, though Sigfrid had said this morning how old-time settlers, one named

99

Champlain, ate tree-bark soup because there were no oranges. We went so fast over drifts that the empty crates kept bouncing off.

Magnus came home after the girls were in bed. I kept watch on the sooty stovepipes, so scared they would overheat and burn us down in our sleep. I must have jumped six inches off my chair when the door breezed open.

Vell, Magnus stamped the snow from his high felt boots, so you survived the blasted storm all right?

His presumption left me speechless.

Look here, he emptied trouser pockets out like elephant ears, I finally vun big.

There were dollar bills galore and several fives, one ten. There wasn't any doubt about his winnings.

Please don't lie to my face, I said with a desperate feeling, the whole town knows how she gets her money.

Ha, Magnus left his money thrown before me, I guess it takes vun to know vun.

My sudden spark of anger kept me from being quite snuffed out.

Isn't she the dainty one, I flared, to be still in her housecoat in the middle of the afternoon! God knows how many men know such a dainty woman.

Ya, he snorted shortly, vell maybe it's time you took your place vith her.

And he yanked me so hard by the hair, I couldn't keep from being led like a dumb beast to the stall.

Slut, I still cried in a whisper, she's a filthy slut who—

He struck me across the mouth, still I went on—slut who gives men diseases—and then I realized he wouldn't care, he'd give me whatever he suffered from too.

Magnus, let go of me, I'm sorry I lost my head, I'm just insane with jealousy.

Ya, he threw me down across the bed, you're insane alright, a crazy hooer like all the rest for me.

His hand was in my breast and then the whole front of my dress was ripped away. I tried to kick where it hurts but he drew down my clothing and twisted my ankle till I thought my whole leg would come off. Then I was so horribly exposed till he stood up on our bed, hauling on my legs just like a wheelbarrow. I had to put a fist in my mouth to keep screams from reaching the girls, oh he was going to

100

finish me this time. *Ffffah* what use to keep my spark alive if my rage set a blaze to consume us? I only wanted my life to raise my girls so they could marry loving men, let my own love go if it had to be taken. And I went so limp he slipped at his critical moment, spilling up my middle toward my face. I couldn't even squirm away, so awful, now I feared I must cry out! Then he dropped with a slap in his mess, forearm ground into my throat, my spattered face pushed up at him.

Ya you sluts are all the same, he whispered fiercely, you could never do vithout me. Don't think you're any different from the girls I used to candydance for in Duluth. Ha you never knew that about me did you Hilda? Ya I used to get girls for sailors, girls you understand who never pretended to be no high and mighty ladies. They knew vy God give 'em a pair of legs and how to use them. Ya, Georgie Halliday, she vas the vun who showed me vat a treasure there is in a voman ha, legs as bowed as a cowboy's and tits like two cherries. She made me vun sveet living, I tell you. I should have left her to stare up a horse's ass.

What hurt me beyond words was not his *horse's ass,* he threw so much worse at me each time his cronies departed. But to be blamed again for knowing about farm life, as if I were only a rump by which a farm was taken—

Then it hit me like a lightning bolt, he *did* marry me to get at Papa's land. And he would have left at once had Banker Loken not beat him at their crooked game. Though what if I had been the one and only *horse's ass?* Oh he must really hate me because he hadn't the stomach to leave me. I listened to him curse under his breath at trouser buttons, unable to do them up right in the dark. His clothes would be so badly stained by his own juices, such a shame to send him off in his mess. But I dare not speak a word.

He went out to the light in the kitchen, I heard him find his pipes and tin of tobacco. He seemed to be hunting for something more, a bottle of rum most likely in the attic or back in the closet. Garments swished in the porch, the outer door creaked, clicked. He was gone.

I got up lamely and found towels to wipe myself. Then I put on my tattered housecoat and went to draw water from the stove. The lamp still burned on the table by the kitchen window.

Uff da I've sat too long and hamstrung myself. But there's no time to lose, I can feel it waiting to be looked at under the bed! I won't wait any more for useless old legs, but crawl, if I must out to my back bedroom.

I blunder through the red curtain, getting tangled like a cow beneath the clothesline. Oh my guts will tumble through my hernia if I kneel any farther! There. There between sheets of cardboard, I can almost feel that old portrait glowing.

Nammen such a pile of lint beneath the bed, I'm ashamed to be caught in my old sins. *Phew* how my old dirt scatters before the bellows. There. *There!*

His face still terrifies me.

One day—how could I forget it? April 16, 1932—we were really in terrible straits to take our eggs to town. We needed fruit and flour and so many other staples. But water was still flowing over the road to the north. We walked down to the foot of the pasture and watched from the knoll.

I think we can get out, I said, if we bring both washtubs.

So we floated ourselves off Tanglewood Island, ferrying to and fro with our bare arms for paddles, nearly freezing in the icy water. And then we used the tubs to cart our egg crates, I with a hand on each in the middle, in case we needed them again. We did. There were seven more fordings in six miles.

We should wait, I said the second time, for the paddleboat to pick us up at Schultzes Landing.

The girls took me seriously. But it was serious business. By the time we got to town our arms were numb from all the weight and chilly water.

Let's stop at the Post Office, I suggested, and rest while we look at our mail.

Mr Dahl at the wicket didn't recognize me, I had to give him my name.

There's just a letter for your husband.

I glanced at a strange red stamp, NORGE arching over the oval of a silhouetted king. There was no hope at all for me to mind my own business.

I went out with girls and egg-tubs into the windswept street. I couldn't contain my excitement. We turned a corner by the Northstar

Theatre and stepped into the lee of wall. Magnus's letter had been re-addressed three times before it got to Canada.

My fingers tore at the flap, heedless of discovery.

Mom, Christine said, what is it? Your face is so white.

The letter was all in *norsk*, the queer Hardanger dialect that Magnus rarely spoke. But no one needed to translate for me a mother's words to her son. Magnus's mother begged him to come home. His father was two months in the grave and how she longed to see her youngest son once more. Could he not come home before she too was called to meet her Maker?

What turned my knees to jelly was the name I hunted out amongst the tearings on the flap. Mrs Kristofer Vangdal, then a scrap ripped away, Hardanger, Norge. *Vangdal.* So my name wasn't even Sigurdson! Oh my whole trust in fate was just a joke, a cruel illusion!

I couldn't lift my end of the tubs.

Girls, I said, please run to where Daddy lives and give him this letter. Tell him—tell him I'm sorry his father has died.

They both looked at me so startled, then Sigfrid snatched the letter. Christine had to fly to stay with her sister's long legs. While they were gone, I took the wooden lids off the crates. Then I carried my liners, one and a half dozen at a time, into the alley behind the theatre and dumped all in the rusty incinerator. I would have tossed in newsprint too if I had the matches for a blaze.

Still his painted likeness looks up at me now with the last laugh. Oh he was within his rights to blame me, I had no right at all to open his letter.

Why don't you send me to jail? I told him. I have nothing left to live for.

That was to be the last time I would ever see him, soon forced himself to flee the threat of prison. He was charged with bookmaking, not what I thought at first—some filth he published about me—but a crime of holding bets for other men. Later I heard some woman from Pathlow had left a husband and three young children to run away with him.

After that I figured the town should let me forget, even if I couldn't myself. But no, the day Papa bought my lot here on the hill and ordered lumber for a house and a shack for himself at the back, different ones, all ladies, came out to the farm to ask what was I doing? They stood in the yard, two or three on tiptoe just to catch a glimpse of me through the screen door. Others looked embarrassed, watching the hens peck and scratch in the dirt.

We'd like to know, Mrs. Benny Pederson said outright, if what we hear is true.

Her wide-brimmed bonnet made her look like a shrivelled sunflower.

I'm afraid it is, I said cool as you please, but I'm sure someone else will come along to take over my egg run. I doubt that deliveries will be interrupted.

Her husband owned the Red & White store and she had always had a sliver because I undersold them.

You know that's not what I mean.

The way so many ladies hung their heads, I could feel sorry for them.

I'm afraid you'll have to tell me, then. I never pay any attention to gossip.

I mean, she drew herself up, that we don't want a separated woman bringing shame on the town.

My hand fumbled in the corner for at least a broom.

Don't you think, I kept my voice quite level, you've shamed yourself enough by coming out here, Mrs. Pederson? Why don't you just go home?

And I pushed the door open, forcing her back. She saw the broom.

You don't threaten me!

Oh but I must, Mrs. Pederson. Else where would you get such nerve?

I felt as light and giddy as the day I'd made my famous curtsey. I might have stepped right off the stoop and walked on air!

Mrs. Pederson gaped like a hen with her neck thrust through chicken wire. Her eyes stopped looking at me, seeing herself lay an egg before so many. Then her hand snatched the broom before I was ready. It made me so mad I shoved her, grabbing back the broom as she tottered. A hand from behind steadied her.

Don't try that again, I panted, or I'll send you for a ride on it!

Her face was dark as the sunflower shorn of its petals.

I'll have you up for assault! You ladies saw her—

Scat! I whisked her shins with the bristles.

When she lunged in stubborn pride again, I whacked her. She yipped like a small dog, turned tail and ran. I swatted at her behind.

The whole bunch scattered at once for the cars. I stayed on Mrs. Pederson's tail till she leaped for the running board of the Ford. Then I stood and laughed to see the car jackrabbit. It stopped at the road, making me nervous. But Mrs. Pederson was only down and squatting in the ditch under the shade of her yellow bonnet. When she did stand up again, I saw her reaching for more brome grass. Then she was squatting and viping ha for all she vas vorth. Oh ha ha ha I vasn't the only horse's ass!

Oh my yes to laugh is to be free again. I can even look at that awful painting I did of Magnus after he left! But it makes me feel bad to think his mouth should look so twisted, laughing on and on in that black void. I don't deny it's how I felt at the time. But surely I belonged in the mental asylum.

I search his painted eyes for a sign that there was something after all in that name he adopted. Did he know what it meant and so chose his fate, or did he borrow it from another sailor and fate took him over? After this long, it still wounds me to think all might have been just his invention. Oh, if I had put my faith in him, believed him to be the great figure he chose to be, why couldn't he be my fate? or why would our love not matter in the scheme of things?

I know he is dead, but that is not the reason these tears are welling. My own heart has given me my verdict, my life not wasted after all. He couldn't pass on without claiming my heart at the final instant.

But my eyes will not take the word of my heart, fixed on that old painting. Something moves and I look up at the red curtain in the doorway. Magnus has just passed through it into my bedroom. He stands there in the same hooded parka he wore that night fifty-eight years ago. I can see the light flicker behind him, just passed through the flames, but his face is not tortured, his mouth so peaceful without its painted scar of laughter. And then I see his eyes so tender look into the unlit corners of my heart. He holds my glance so quietly, so yearningly. Then simply disappears.

My whole face melts down in a great flood. I can feel it pouring beneath me on my way out to the living room. Blind fingers grope again for the knob on the stereo, and I set the arm as lightly as I can upon the black hole of the record. Then Brünnhilde's voice takes up my trials again, but on a plane beyond all my pain.

II
LOKI

Christine

The night nurse tries to spare me from draining Daddy's ostomy pouch.

"Why don't you go see your family in the T.V. room?" she says sweetly. "Take a little breather, if you'll pardon the expression."

We smile sadly at this joke against the flesh, mothers both of us who have lost sons born of our flesh. After a week Mrs Whitely told me about her Philip's death and how, for a time, she couldn't come back inside a hospital. But families are knit together by powers stronger than death.

"Honestly, Mrs Goodman, you should get some rest. They say in the staff room you've been here since the morning shift. You know you can't go on like this day after day..."

Her voice trails off hurt by the thought that nothing else might be done for him, it is now out of reach of human hands. I look at her with neither hope nor unhope, her face is careworn from attendance at so many of life's last scenes. Finally all reluctance dies out of her eyes, her cap nods slightly as she turns the sheet back from Daddy's mutilated side. Both his hands flutter up like my babies' used to do when I would unwrap them in their sleep. Now the shining bedpan is blurred by my tears, I can't control myself for a moment, finally I can see to fit its wide mouth onto the bag sealed to his stomach.

The odour, as Mrs Whitely undoes the clamp, takes my breath away, it is tinged more surely than ever with the fact of his death. I know the smell is not from him, it is the stench of the cancer. But my big, strong husband turned stark white under his nose the last time the gas erupted. Sigfrid followed him out, I asked her to see to him in case he needed me. I was afraid she would stay by Daddy's side till she vomited again.

New wind breaks from the hole, liquid squirts violently against the plastic. Then it is streaming so ghastly down inside the pan, great gusts of it spattering the mouth. I try to press the pan up farther without hurting him. Mrs Whitely shakes her head, I draw it down again, she sticks her hand into the torrent and reclamps the pouch. Still the clots of matter swirl and boil within the bag. The blood is bitten from her nether lip as she looks up, her eyes tell me the moment has come. It is my turn to nod. She goes out the door on the dead run.

I clutch at Daddy's long fingers, and unbelievably they clench and clasp my own. Then I am startled to see him staring up at me, his eyes like a room unveiled. I am glad of that, I am strangely glad for him, how his eyes brim clear and clean. My sister must see him too as he looks back on us over the threshold of death.

"Sigfrid," I cry out, though my heart is not afraid. Daddy's eyes burn brighter still. Then I hear the clatter of heels on the hallway tile, and Sigfrid comes bursting in with Garney close behind. She looks, for all her slender five-foot-eleven, like a little girl again. I remember how stricken she looked that morning Mother was asleep in her chair by the wood-stove. Sigfrid's eyes were just struck, it had never occurred to her that Daddy would leave us.

"Daddy," she rushes to the near side of the bed, "Daddy, don't go so soon..."

Her lips twitch uncontrollably. Now he must tell her that he loves her, poor Sigfrid has tried to blame herself too long for what happened. But none of us could help it, it was meant to be. No wonder her nerves have been so bad, just a word from him might now cure her awful migraines. I press his hand with all my heart.

"I leave you ..." Daddy struggles to make himself heard above the gush of the ostomy "...all my vordly goods" ...he speaks directly to Sigfrid now, really a kind of love at last "...a real pile ha."

110

But his bout of self-mockery leaves him winded, he pants tremendously for breath. Oh he cannot get air, his pupils swim to points! At once the gush of waste is stopped. Then his eyes float back to us, he wills himself to stay and speak some more. I grip his great hand, signalling him to rest. He gulps the precious air. The last button on his pyjamas bursts, the nurses had to shave him shamefully this morning so the tape on his pouch wouldn't pull. When we were children he always took such care to have his face smoothshaven, he would rise well before daylight to light a fire in the stove. And we would lie there with frost in our hair, our noses hid beneath the quilt, smiling to hear him sing in Norwegian to the kitchen mirror. We were always so pleased until we found out what the words meant.

"Daddy," Sigfrid's eyes shine like the sun through a mist, "Daddy, what worldly goods do you mean? For heaven's sake, don't mock us any more."

"...my old sea-chest" the word bursts from him, oh it is the gas exploding from his side, spurting with such a vengeance! "...thousands, ya...a real fortune....I vant to do vat's right...."

His voice pours out the hole in his side, I have only a moment to catch him. I had hoped all along he might say it for himself.

"Daddy, don't you have a word for Mama that will cheer her?"

But his eyes drain toward the bottom, life goes swirling out, he is gone.

"Daddy," Sigfrid tugs at his hand.

The doctor in rubber-soled shoes comes swiftly through the door. He sees my face, then slows so he will not interfere with Sigfrid. Mrs Whitely, poor soul, puffs along behind. I feel some pressure now from Daddy's fingers though he is released from all his pain. Below me the bladder collects what remains yet under pressure. Sigfrid looks at it in surprise, then disgust, beginning to weep. Gently the doctor draws her aside. Now he takes out his pocketlight and raises one of Daddy's eyelids.

Garney gives me such a loving look, I nearly burst into tears myself. And then I can't help it, another death scene lives again before my eyes. I am kneeling in the street where my child's life drains into the dirt. I can't bring myself to look behind his ear, clotted with gore, where the wheel drove over his head. I sit in the gravel before our store and take up his yellow curls in my lap, soaking what remains of his life into my clean dress. He must have been trying to get his ball from behind the wheel when ...Mrs Delgatty couldn't help it, poor soul, I mustn't blame her for being so rackety about her grief.

Dear me, it is Daddy who is dead and Sigfrid now who's hysterical.

"Sweetheart," I reach out to her. But she shrinks from being comforted.

The doctor completes his examination of Daddy's eyes. He looks across at Mrs Whitely who has abandoned the search for any pulse.

"He's dead," he says quietly to Garney and to me.

I nod through the veil of my tears.

"We'll leave you alone for as long as you want," he says understandingly. "Mrs Whitely will be back when you're ready ..."

The doctor steps aside, Mrs Whitely puts her hand gently to Sigfrid's arm which has become clamped to the rail of the bed. Sigfrid looks up through her tears, struggling to get hold of herself. She nods that she's alright, but as soon as the nurse goes, she turns back as in a dream to the body. I shudder as she catches Daddy's hand up to her cheek, so horribly stained! But the blood cannot be sunk down as yet, that is why the liver spots stand out. I really mustn't interfere when this is the only chance she has to get the blessing she missed in his life.

I glance at Garney sitting in the chair by the door, he feels my eyes on him and stands up quietly. I steal along the bed toward the foot of the corpse, saying my last goodbyes in spirit. Garney takes my hand as we step out into the glaring light. I am grateful for his steady strength beside me. Part of my life lies behind me there, oh it hurts to be separated so soon again!

Sigfrid's voice rises like a wail behind us. "You're not going without me?"

I look back to reassure her. Hastily she composes Daddy's hands on his breast. Then she almost runs at us, she is much too tall to have to run for anything.

"I'm sorry," I say, but my voice sounds shaky, I will have to be stronger for her sake. "We only want to give you a moment together, I know how much he cared for you."

"At least he made us both his heirs," she says in a choked voice. She's still bothered by the bad air. "Though of course it wouldn't be like him, would it, to name us in a will?"

112

I remember to breathe the fresh air again, oh I was feeling so faint from having to take those shallow breaths!

"You don't really think," Garney says slowly, "that there's any money where he said?"

"You wouldn't call a dead man a liar, would you?"

"Of course not, Sigfrid, but don't you think—well, where would he get it from? You saw how he lived, he had no pension from Cominco."

"My father said he left thousands," Sigfrid answers shortly. "Don't think you'll get me off the track of it."

Garney looks sideways at me. I haven't the heart left to speak, the floor is heaving up at me.

"Good Lord," I hear him say from far away, then darkness rushes close around me ....

....such hideous faces leer, before they slip back into darkness to jeer at me unseen. I can feel my arms bound to a throne where thick ropes hold my feet quite fast. Then the faces mob me again. One of them seems to be Daddy's, but it is so twisted, it couldn't be him at all!

Garney's dear face looks down out of the bright halo of lights. He is gravely concerned, I think I might have been dreaming again that awful nightmare, the one I have dreamed since childhood, though I can never recall it. Something tightens on my arm, I want to scream. Out of the corner of my eye I catch the nurse chafing at my wrist. Dear Mrs Whitely, I must have fainted, I remember panting so hard to get my breath.

"Just lie back," Mrs Whitely says soothingly. "You've played yourself right out."

Garney nods his approval, neither of them would ever say I told you so.

"Where is Sigfrid?" I ask keenly.

Sigfrid's face appears almost at once over the foot of the bed. She pats my instep thoughtfully, the muscles of her jaw a-work. "You've let yourself get the flu, Christine. They want to keep you in here."

"Don't worry about me," I sit up in one motion. "I really am all right. Garney, can't we go home now? There's so much to be done in the morning—"

He looks at me with surprise and relief, he always did hate to go to sleep alone. I couldn't bear to have him take a hotel room for the night, it would be such a waste of money when Daddy's place has the two bedrooms.

Mrs Whitely looks embarrassed.

"The doctor can't be held responsible if you go."

"Thank you," I say sadly. "I don't mean to cause you any trouble. But Sigfrid needs me, don't you see?" I look at Garney whose eyes are faintly troubled.

"Really," the nurse smiles like my guardian angel, "I don't know what to do with you, Mrs Goodman. Get you a job on the ward, I suppose, so you won't run yourself to—"

She stops in time, my eyes tell her how much I appreciate her tact.

"Promise me," she says in reply, "that you'll sleep when you get home. And Mrs Goodman...try not to think of little Charles tonight. You know that your father is really....Well, things are finally as they should be."

I try to smile my thanks.

We pass down the yellow hallway to the nurse's station. I will not think tonight about his yellow curls. Sigfrid is nowhere in sight.

"No," Garney puts his foot down at the exit to the stairwell, "we're going to take the elevator, I don't care if it is one flight to the lobby."

We pass out of the elevator in front of the gift shop, it was closed hours ago, I meant to buy some pictures of Trail for Mother. Garney says it is cheaper to buy post cards than to use our own camera, that way we will have professional photographs done in bright weather.

Sigfrid waits between the glass doors, she is staring out at an empty taxi stand. Her bootheel frets outward so nervously, I think she might really have spent the money on a taxi. It hurts me to see her without a husband, she ought to enjoy the warmth and support of a family of her own. But she could never bring herself to marry. Every time I hinted at her prospects in a city the size of Saskatoon, she said flatly she was wed to her music.

"I'm sorry we've been so long," I say to her thin cloth coat. Blue is not her best colour, it makes her look so ashen.

But the way she looks at me, I know she hasn't been thinking of the time. Pain is like a lamp behind her eyes.

"Sigfrid," my heart goes out to her, "he loved you, you know. You don't have to prove it. He loved you, there's no way to measure it, love is all-embracing."

"*Omnia vincit amor*," she says bitterly. I don't know what she means, she sees my doubt. "The jacket crests they wear nowadays at Nisooskan Collegiate, have you never seen them?" But I didn't go as far as high school, I worked as a hired girl after Sigfrid went to Saskatoon. Uncle Peder and Aunt Loretta could only afford to keep one of us, things were so terribly expensive in the city. "Love conquers all," the bitterness surfaces in her voice once more. "Well, I wasn't one of his conquests, was I?"

"I'll bring the car round," Garney says swiftly to fill up the silence.

"It's not that far, is it?" I try to sound cheerful. We can all walk together.

He takes my arm and we leave the U-shaped foyer behind us. The snow is sopping down like wet pillowfeathers.

Sigfrid doesn't speak when Garney opens the door for her. I reach across the seat to lift his latch. Her bootheel frets, she shrinks from the touch of my knee.

We back away from the rock wall, I turn to look one last time at the lettering in the bay, TRAIL REGIONAL HOSPITAL. Thank goodness we found Daddy before it was too late! Sigfrid stares straight ahead, it hurts her to think Daddy is no longer there.

The lights of the hospital wink out, we plunge after our own headlights through the cut in the hill. I am afraid to look at what lies beneath us! But we do not spin out of control, Garney slows through all the turns until we roll onto the valley floor. Up on the plateau beyond the river stands the smelter with its running lights on, I can't quite see the smokestacks through the snowstorm. I remember the day I first caught sight of it from the window of the hospital. It made me think of a steamship with three funnels and a great prow rising out of the water. I don't know why it made me feel so small, like a dwarf or a pygmy.

The bridge arches above us, I feel the emptiness below as the tires begin to hum on steel. All those times Sigfrid and I walked across the bridge before Garney came out, I never dared look over the rail. The rush of so much water threatened to sweep me away. But Garney steers with such steady hands over the void that we re-enter the land of the living.

Just past the sign of Jezebel's Discotheque we swerve left to run up the mountain. Dearest mother, she suffered so because of all those wicked women.

115

Daddy's apartment is dark. Oh he is gone, the ache in my breast tells me, gone from this wicked world, gone to rest with the ages! The car rolls to a stop on Hendry Street.

Garney switches the engine off, then waits for one of us to do something. The way his hands grip the steering wheel, I see what a strain this has been on him too. Perhaps we ought not go back, after all, to sleep inside that house. Sigfrid stirs as from a deeper sleep, then flings right out of the car. For a moment I am left spellbound.

"Sigfrid," I call into the scurry of snowflakes, "wait, you mustn't go in there alone!"

But she is already searching in her purse for the key to the porch door. I rush across the trestle to be with her, here the hill falls away save for the lower part of the house beneath me. As I clatter like a Billy Goat Gruff, Sigfrid glances over her shoulder. Now she grimaces in fear of the empty room beyond.

"It's all right, Sigfrid," I pant for breath, "we'll face it together."

Garney's heavy step hits the plank behind us, the whole walkway trembles. His full, round face glistens in the streetlight with such damp concern. I look at his tummy bulging through his jacket, it isn't good for him to run so hard. I reach out to take his gloved hand, reassuring him with a glance. Sigfrid's hand fumbles round the doorpost. The light falls like a caress over her fair hair. Oh I will not think of those shining yellow curls!

The room is cold as the—space-heater must have gone out. Garney kneels before it, he knows how to get it running again.

Now Sigfrid stares at me with such heart-breaking hope. "It's not the money, Christine, you can have it all if you want. I only want him to keep his word to us."

I am flabbergasted to think—"Sigfrid, I don't want a penny from Daddy, I only mean to help you bear it when we—"

Sigfrid pushes her bottom teeth out till the plate pops up. Her lower mouth is so empty that I look away in confusion.

"Come on then," her plate is out of sight again, "we might as well face the music."

Daddy's storage room is nothing but a hole in the wall beneath the eaves.

"You pull," Sigfrid looks back at me, "and I'll get in there and push."

She stoops to pull an apple-box filled with books around her leg, I cart it out the door. It is the same *B.C. Macs* label that we stock in our store at home. Again, another case of books, I never knew Daddy to be so interested in reading! Then it hurts to think that I should know so little about him. Better, perhaps, not to know too much.

Sigfrid doesn't wait, she opens a little tin suitcase in the space she has cleared. Her mouth, as she looks back at me, is a hole filled with sorrow.

"That's not it," I say quietly, my heart beats so hard against my ribs I can't breathe again, "not his—seaman's chest."

Her spine jolts straight. For a moment she seems to have grasped a bare wire, her head bumps on the rafters! Then the sound of her throwing up comes almost as a relief!

"Here, honey," I thrust my ragged kleenex at her, no time even to remove the lint from my pocket, "come out of there, it isn't good for you to see such things." She has never had to handle anything like a child's diarrhea. Diapers have helped me get ready for this. There lies one of Daddy's ostomy pouches in a pool of dirt on the floor. His stool is scattered down the wall between the studs, then right up over the top of his sailor's chest.

"You poor dear," I dab with my remaining kleenex at her mouth till her chin comes clean. "Come out here and rest on the chesterfield."

Sigfrid sits obediently while I help her off with her coat. Garney ambles out from the kitchen looking pleased with himself.

"I've got the oven heating— What on earth—?"

"She found a mess— " I hate to speak as if she weren't even here, "Daddy left a bit of mess in there."

Garney's eyes twinkle as if he would make light of it. I tell him with my eyes, "She feels bad enough, you don't want to humiliate her."

He shrugs and goes back to the tiny kitchen, I can hear him running water in the plastic garbage pail. I mop swiftly at Sigfrid's fingers, dear soul, she tried so hard to hold it in. Some of it has run up her sleeve, she should get it off and soak it, it's the only new dress she owns and such a lovely pink taffeta.

"You've got your marching orders," I say when she gets up to help. "Go change your clothes or I'll send you to bed."

Garney comes back with a bundle of old rags. I catch a whiff of Mr Clean in his bucket. Now Sigfrid goes as she is bid to her bedroom.

"*Nammen,*" I say to my husband, "that will be the day I let you do woman's work."

The splashes that Daddy left on the wall are quite bad, I feel my whole gorge rise as I kneel down. Then I am all right, I scrub like a trooper. Finally there is only the major thing left. His sea-chest has taken the brunt of it. I reach out with my wringing-wet cloth, then draw back at once. Oh, it used to horrify me so beneath their bed, the sight of it was worse than of the huge, rubber-bulbed things in Mother's dresser drawer. Daddy didn't have to tell me not to touch it.

I wipe the brass bands over the hump, they are so fouled by time's corruption that they might never be cleansed. But the last of Daddy's stool wipes easily from the wood. Now why do I feel faint when the worst is done? I was so sure it was just the closeness of the hospital room when he—! I must back out of here, I drag the chest as I go like some old miser reluctant to let go.

"Good night nurse!" Garney gets after me from the doorway. He is right, it will soon be lights out for me if I don't quit! I drop the leather handle, beginning to feel myself like a balloon going up.

Garney catches me under my arms. Oh I'm not going to faint, I fight to look up! I see—that chest, it terrifies me so! Still this awful groan is not my own, it comes from right above me. I must have frightened the wits out of my dear husband!

"I'm all right," I say faintly, "the trunk just got too heavy for me. I hope I didn't bother the people in the apartment below, dropping it like that."

For answer, he sweeps me up like a bride before a threshold.

"Garney, I'm too heavy for you." Then I see the ache in Sigfrid's eyes, watching us from her bedroom door. "Put me down," I whisper, "for Sigfrid's sake, put me down!"

He blushes like a boy. I have never stopped loving that boy in him. Then I get my legs again. It would be so easy to go to bed, but Sigfrid's eyes are like two black holes.

"It's there, Sigfrid," I point with such a heavy finger, my arm must be weighed down by leaden digits.

"Please bring it into the light," she barely breathes, "I feel so weak."

"You feel—" Garney says in choked surprise, then stoops abruptly. The trunk comes bouncing out of the cubby-hole like a runaway buggy. I feel the terrible tension around us. Sigfrid is bound to get a migraine if I don't speak out.

"It's my fault," I say truthfully, "I let myself go kind of queer again."

"She almost fainted," Garney's voice relents a little.

"Maybe you'd rather wait for morning, Christine?" She tries to hide a sudden eagerness.

"I wouldn't sleep." I wouldn't dare to sleep. Oh, I am doomed if I do, doomed if I don't!

"Damned," Sigfrid says matter-of-factly. Was I thinking aloud then? But she pays me no mind, fumbling already with the brass snap-locks. The button depresses, the tongue flicks out—

Oh my unwilling heart—but it is bare! Bare as Mother Hubbard's cupboard!

"What's this?"

Sigfrid snatches up a sheet of newsprint lining, her lip quivering with sorrowful excitement. Then I try to read over her shoulder. It is a newspaper picture of Daddy in his younger days, wearing a miner's hat and holding up a terrible-looking drill. The caption is something about lease miners, they have given up looking for gold in the Leroi Mine. I search for a date, the paper is from 1942, almost half his life ago.

"He left us a clue," Sigfrid pants, "he couldn't let us down after all, not at the very end."

But I can't face the agony of hope in her voice. Garney wants to see it too but Sigfrid clutches it like a relic. He politely turns away to the trunk and comes up with a sheet of his own.

"This is strange," he says with mild curiosity, "he packed his trunk with a Moose Jaw *Times-Herald*. Look, the headlines are about the Lindbergh kidnapping. Now why would he do that?"

"Mother knew Charles Lindbergh," I have to say, but the words nearly get away on me. "Daddy was jealous of any man she used to know."

"You're kidding, your Mother knew Charles Lindbergh? Why didn't you tell me?"

From somewhere I hear Sigfrid say, "She saw him land in a neighbour's pasture, that's all. He was just a Minnesota boy, you know. He worked for a farmer on our side of the Red River."

119

"I'll be doggoned. But what would your Dad be doing in Moose Jaw? That's a part of his past I never heard about."

I feel myself going, it is like I have to shout back from a great distance. "It was the winter he left us . . . probably on his way out to Trail . . . ."

"Good lord, girl," he says, "you're pale as— You've got to climb right into the sack!"

The strength of his hand flows into me, I come back after all, gladly suffering myself to be led like the lamb. Then he is unhooking my dress, I put up my arms like a little child, oh he is taking it off to slip my nightgown on, where can it be? But he forgets to take off my bra. I will lie down in spite of how it binds.

"Here," he says so gently, he has returned from somewhere, "here is the sleeping pill the doctor ordered."

It is a glass of water he puts into my hand, now he puts the pill between my lips. My mouth relaxes, I don't want to sleep, I try to hide the pill beneath my tongue.

"Swallow," my good man says, "that's it, swallow a little more water."

He is undressed in a moment, I catch sight of his stout middle in the blue boxer shorts. His face seems so grave before the light goes out. I am lying on my side, then the pill oozes out of my mouth. Garney slips beneath the covers and brushes my neck with a kiss. I close my eyes, recalling our bed at home when Sigfrid and I were little, before sleep turned to nightmare. Oh it seems so long since I had a good night's rest, all those many years ago. I remember how I used to snuggle with my back to her, both our heads under the covers, and how quickly we'd get warm just by breathing hard. And I would think how I must not think, I must empty myself of each scene brimming over from the day. Then in time every picture would swim out from behind my eyes, leaving no impression, nothing outside the growing circle of the dark. And then I was dropping down, still farther down, through that final, restful dark.

A hand steals over the window-sill, the foot and leg climb first into the room. Daddy stands above the bed, Sigfrid is still snoring away at my back. Daddy takes a bit of rope from the bib of his overalls, I feel the cord slide under my head. There is no use crying out, I have to open my eyes and wait, watching him so near above me. Something makes him look at me, the rope drops like a lit match from his fingers. I hear him moan with hurt, now his eyes speak a love greater than the death in his heart. We gaze at one another for an age, it seems. He knows I love him too.

"Goodbye my sveet," he whispers, stooping to brush my forehead with his lips. For an instant I see him framed by the sill, then the moon flashes on Charles's yellow curls. The baby is passed to other hands, now the window is empty.

Still I wait as I have waited before for him to return through the door. North Portal they say it is on the radio. But he is hiding out with his gang in Devil's Lake. The radio says they are expected to cross the border on their way toward Moose Jaw. Mother cries and cries each time we hear about the kidnapping. One day Sigfrid asks her, "Why aren't you crying as hard for Daddy?" and Mother, who is wiping her eyes with one of Daddy's red hankies, cries out as though her heart is broken. I creep against her knees, she gathers me into a cloud of talc and lilac water, then Sigfrid joins our tight little circle. For a time we all howl. "My, that poor Ann Lindbergh," Mother dries her eyes at last, "to be as helpless as that, not able to do a thing for her bab—" but her voice breaks, I feel her sorrow like a stain on my heart. I try to tell her Daddy wouldn't harm him, he only wants the money. I know for a fact he wouldn't harm a child.

The days drag on, we hear how the Lindbergh representatives are dealing in secret with some agents who sound more desperate by the day. Ann Lindbergh is seen in a window, she is smiling, they say, there is hope in Hopewell, New Jersey. Then the news breaks, the kidnappers have grabbed the fifty thousand dollars and kept the baby. The money has been paid in a far-off New York cemetery. I ask Mother how far it is from North Dakota to New York City. She says, "Why do you ask?" Then I know my sorrow is my own, I must not add one stick to the load of her suffering.

We sit numbly by the radio in our tiny living room, we have just heard that the baby is dead, we don't know how or when. Still I am surprised how grief can seem so much like peace. The words that should have smashed like hammer blows have missed their mark. The baby was dead before his parents missed him. Oh, our hope was empty before there was even reason to hope!

Still I will not think of that little head, broken in the woods by the murderer's hammer. But I remember thinking with my own boy in my arms, We have paid, dear god, how we have paid! Poor Wayne, I know he would have taken the blame himself if he could. No one loved his brother more than he did, he saw it all from half a block away, and rode his bike shouting at her to stop. I would have gladly died for both my boys, but there was nothing I could do any more for little Charles, it was Wayne who needed all my love. I cradled his head where he knelt with his cheek against his brother's little cheek.

"It couldn't be helped," I murmured over and over, "there's a curse on our family."

Mother said the same thing when we left the hospital at last to break the news to her. Garney stayed in the car with Wayne and the girls. Mother searched my face through an instant of disbelief.

"Oh, there must be a curse on us," she whispered, till we hugged our grief between us.

Dear me, have I been dreaming that awful dream again? The window must be faint with the dawn, grey skies for another day. I try not to wake Garney as I steal past the foot of the bed.

There's a huge scatter of books on the living room floor, I don't want to tread on them. Sigfrid must have been too tired to clean up after herself. Some of the books, when I pick them up, fall apart, leaving nothing at all between their covers. Sigfrid is liable to have a terrible migraine today, poor soul.

But in the dark it is really Wayne I am reaching for with every book I pick up. Surely the university would have given him leave to visit his dying grandfather. He hated to have to go anywhere with me, I suppose. He has never forgiven me for coming between him and Karen. I don't know how I could have acted so foolishly ... At least I gained a daughter if I had to lose my other son as well .... I can only pray that one day he might understand and forgive. Though it scares me to think he'd rather be free of us ...so much like Daddy....

At last I can see my way clear to the kitchen. I try not to mind the trunk yawning open. If the ransom is hidden away in all these books, we might restore that much, at least, to the Lindbergh heirs. I tiptoe through the tiny room, hesitating to close the lid on the trunk, so dreadful to my touch last night. There, There's room enough to get by.

The kitchen light-switch snaps too loudly. I blink in the glare from a bare light bulb. The walls don't help to dim it, they are a glossy cream colour, except for the stains. The few pictures had to be taken down, better to look at bare walls than so many pictures of bare women. Daddy always wanted mother to paint like that. And now even the better magazines have to print such junk.

I spread the letter tablet on the rickety table. But after some time, I see I am still staring at a blank page. I must be dozing, there will be time for sleep when we go home again. I try to get hold of my thoughts.

17 January 1978

Dearest Mother,

We were by Daddy's side last night when he died. I can't say it was an easy death, you know what cancer is like, but he faced it openly and honestly—

Floorboards creak. I look up at Sigfrid in the doorway, she stands with a hand to the side of the hump-backed fridge.

I say, "What's wrong?"

Her face is as drawn as any graven image.

"I didn't sleep a wink." Her eyelids are red, she has been crying too.

"You poor dear, I was worried when I saw your covers. What can I get you?"

"Nothing. I should take an aspirin before it gets worse."

I go to the cupboard, I'm pretty sure it's here and not in the bathroom.

"Christine, what are you doing? You sit. I'm a big girl, I can look after myself."

I hand her the glass of water. She nearly drops the aspirin out of my palm, her hand is shaking so hard.

"What are you doing," she murmurs with the aspirin tablet in her mouth, "up this early?"

"I wanted to write to Mother, I was finished sleeping. Sigfrid, I didn't mean to go to sleep on you last night, but Garney—the nurse—"

"Don't always try to blame yourself."

She glances down at the floor. When her eyelids rise again, there shines, as with the graciousness of indirect lighting, a subdued hope.

"I—I think I was kind of crazy last night," she confesses shyly. I start to shake my head, but she prevents me. "No—I really was, I was sitting like a child on the living room floor, and I was breaking the spines on those books and relishing it. I wasn't even looking for bills tucked away. I was cracking the spines to hear spines crack. Oh Christine, you don't know what it's like to feel you're such a Jezebel —"

"Ha," I must be grinning like a dog in my relief, "I do every time we pass that disco place—"

"You—?" Sigfrid gasps, and then she snorts, we are both snorting and choking together till we collapse in one another's arms.

"Oh," I draw in my breath at last, "oh my, but it does feel good to go crazy now and then."

"I hope you're right. What did you write to Mother?"

"I was only getting started. Would you like to take over?"

"No. I have to get dressed. I might add a few lines when you're finished."

But when she is gone, I don't know what to say. I have to comfort Mama somehow. Yet I can't lie.

> Daddy knew how much he'd wronged you, dearest Mama. But he suffered too in the end. We might take some comfort in the hope that all our pain had a common purpose. It is meant to undo a great wrong, and we will bear that wrong a little further, if only to realize his good inten—

"How can you say such a thing?" Sigfrid says sharply over my shoulder.

"Oh dear, you startled me."

"You know he couldn't care less how she felt. He must be laughing right now in hell—"

Then her lips twitch with the effort not to cry.

"I didn't know how else to spare her feelings, Sigfrid."

For an instant her face is clouded, then it is just like the sun coming out.

"Maybe you're right. It's barely possible he'd have left us something to go on. We shouldn't give up yet."

"Would you like some coffee?" I say lamely.

"Love some. Why don't you let me make it?"

"You work on Mother's letter. You can say it better than I can."

While I spoon the grounds into Daddy's stained steel pot, I watch her head bent in earnest over the table.

Nammen! Here I've forgotten and opened up the bread box! It's been filled, since the day we got here, with awful, crawling things that I dare not touch. Oh, I don't know what we'll have to eat now. I close the lid carefully, putting a stack of dishes on it. That way Sigfrid won't be tempted to open it.

She crumples the letter in one swift motion.

"It's just not possible," she scowls. Then her eyes grow gentle as she spies my face. "Don't you remember what Mama always said? 'If you can't say something nice, say nothing at all.' "

I nod, hearing the coffee begin to bump on the stove. Garney won't like it that I've gotten up without him. The front room looks, in the growing light, like a battlefield. I am drawn, as always in the day, to the view of the mountains through the window. Light is beginning to glow along the coal-black range. Its quiet spine could almost be that lady on the TV commercial, resting on her side in the dark until the light breaks over the ridge, not mountains at all that you'd let yourself believe in, but a person lying on that mattress for money. I suppose there are women bustling in all the bright-lit houses to get their husbands off to work in the smelter. Did Daddy ever miss Mother, I wonder, on days when he got up alone?

Then I find I am not watching where the river pours straight-away. My eyes beat back instead around the bend, under both bridges, to the point where a steamship rides at landing, its huge funnels still smoking lightly—

Oh, I must hurry, I'm starting to hallucinate. They say if you don't sleep your brain will dream awake. The bedroom door squeaks, then I see Garney is still sound asleep. He lies on his tummy like Wayne did when he was a baby. Now where is that clean white blouse? The lock snaps when I close the suitcase. Garney turns his head.

"I'm sorry," I try to put on the blouse as if for the first time, "did I wake you?"

125

He looks at me with pouting lips, he is often grumpy first thing in the morning.

"What's all the hurry?" he says sleepily. "There can't be a fire sale this early."

My hand shakes with such weariness that I put down my wool suit-top, sure to spill something on it if I wear it. Still it's a dark navy . . . .

Garney sits up abruptly, looking like a chastened bear.

"Gosh, Chris, I'm sorry. You know I didn't mean—"

"Silly you, it's not such a bad idea. Funeral homes could learn to do business like the rest of us. Don't you go spending a lot of money on me either when I'm gone."

"Don't worry, I'm going to use the money to take some young thing to Hawaii in the winter."

"I'd rather have that than you moping after me."

"I bet you would. You'd outlive me by twenty years to be on the safe side."

He cocks his head when a chair scrapes in the kitchen.

"How long have you people been up?"

"Just a little while. The coffee is perking, you'd better get dressed before we Norwegians get started."

"Chris," Garney's voice is suddenly so gentle, "are you sure you're rested? You look worn out. Listen, I can go down to the funeral home alone, or maybe with Sigfrid. I can do anything that needs to be done. You could stay here and get some rest—"

"I feel fine," I say truthfully. "It's Sigfrid who's—got another migraine today."

I force a smile and hurry to the kitchen. On the table, two mugs of coffee have been poured. But Sigfrid is about to take my stack of plates off the breadbox!

"Don't open that filthy thing, it's crawling with vermin!"

Sigfrid's hand starts back as if she's touched a red-hot stove. An odd look steals into her eyes.

"Christine, what's wrong? You look like you've seen—something."

Oh, I have been acting strangely. I feel so—hurried.

"I don't know what's come over me. Come on, we've got to settle this sea-chest business."

Sigfrid finishes stirring milk into her coffee. "It's such a relief to see I'm not the only one gone off her rocker." And smiles at me over a cup held just below her lip.

I fight my urge to ransack the place. Still it sweeps under me like the river rushing out of the mountains. Was this the kind of feeling that overcame Sigfrid last night? I wouldn't break backs...none but my own, anyway, to do what's right by him. I force myself to hold the milk carton steady and pour a few drops. But I empty it instead. Now Garney will have none. I don't know why I'm so rattled, I will set my mug aside for him and take an unused one from the cupboard. Sigfrid is out there already, sifting through the mess!

Daddy's books are a jumble, I never liked to read myself, and her I thought I got that from him. I guess I still don't know him after all—but the thought is like the edge of a cliff, I back away. I try to concentrate on the books themselves, some gaudy pocket books, murder mysteries, a few romances ...*Sweet Savage Love*. Daddy had to be lonely at times, I never would have thought— There is nothing else hidden here.

Sigfrid reaches for the last glued tablets on the floor. I have only some vacant covers to add to her carton.

"Well," she says grimly, "we have only about six suitcases and half-a-dozen boxes to go. Then we'll start ripping out the floorboards."

We sift doggedly through boxes of old clothing, pry open old lamps to see if the bills are stashed there. We even tap for false bottoms in the valises ... nothing. We have surrounded ourselves with a heap of junk. I have even stopped bracing for the first sight of blood money, bracing instead for ... I don't know what. Sigfrid's disappointment is keen. I don't know which would disappoint her more—not to know, or to have to find out.

"Man," Garney is here now, loading up the last two cardboard valises, "I sure could use some breakfast soon."

Sigfrid crabs backward to the sea-chest near the doorway. My heart skips a beat when she reaches inside and raps a hollow bottom.

"Aha!" she cries out, plunging like a diver.

By the time I peer over her shoulder, she has a crack along one edge. Then the whole bottom springs to one side, revealing ... Nothing! There is nothing whatsoever in the inch of space below the false bottom!

Sigfrid's teeth pop out again. For a moment I am scared she's going to choke on them. Then she jumps up and races into the kitchen. I don't blame her, though my own feeling of emptiness is so different. I don't know how we could lay Daddy in his grave without acquitting him somehow of his life.

"Eeeee—" Sigfrid shrieks with fright or elation, what has she found? Oh what will I tell her? Then the crash of smashing crockery brings Garney to his feet as quickly as me. I can barely squeeze by him in the doorway . . . . Sigfrid stands discovered with her hand in the breadbox, her outrage changing to a sheepish grin.

She blurts, "The way you snapped at me— Well I couldn't help but think—"

"Oh—oh—oh," I can't get my breath for the peals of laughter, "you thought—you thought—those vermin—" but I am roaring as if a dam has burst. Something pulls in me like a maelstrom, I could really flow right out of myself—

I barely hold back, I will not let go completely. The sight of Sigfrid comes back through my tears, she is crowing now too in spite of her chagrin.

"Oh Sigfrid, I was trying to—to—protect you, not to—cheat you."

Just the thought of it sends me into gales of laughter again. Sigfrid clings to me now, saving me from being swept away.

"Oh ho ho, hee hee," I wash up in waves to where Garney waits on solid ground, "oh, she thought I was stashing Daddy's money in the breadbox with—maggots!"

Sigfrid and I are both convulsed once more. Garney has to laugh at the sight of us. Then a tide of sanity begins to flow beneath the ebb of all our giddiness.

"Well," Garney grins, "I can be glad, at least, that your Dad didn't ask for an Irish wake. The obsequies would kill you."

We get our coats and head outside at last. The clouds hang like a shroud over the face of the mountain. We climb up the icy steps, clinging to the handrail. I feel a curtain lifted in the grey stucco wall overhead, I don't look up.

Garney goes ahead to start the car, it is not plugged in as it would have to be at home. Sigfrid and I idle arm in arm out to the sidewalk. The sound of a motor starting in forty below at home is like a dying groan. I stoop into the back seat to dig out the windshield scraper.

"Here, let me do that," Garney looks over his shoulder.

"I want to, the air is so mild this morning."

Sigfrid stays out here with me, she stamps her boots in the snow like a little girl.

I glance at Daddy's apartment below the house, and the empty space below that. I had hoped his last words wouldn't be empty, now I don't know what to do. Still the thawing winter air makes me hope against hope.

We get in the car at last, the three of us huddling against this feeling of emptiness, and drive to where the snowy road falls away. We go down in a series of bumps as Garney pumps the brakes. Sigfrid braces with mittened hands against the dash. We skid once in a tight right-hand turn, but Garney eases us out, then we are free and in sight of our breakfast.

Jezebel's, I notice for the first time, is part of a four-storey motel, the *Terra Nova*. As we enter the lot, I wonder again what on earth brought Daddy here, was it just a place to hide, or did he stay in hope of something else among these mountains?

"Aren't you coming?" Garney says suddenly, he is leaning back inside the car. "Chris, aren't you feeling well?"

"I'm fine." I slide off the benchseat as fast as I can. "I've been trying to puzzle out Daddy's mystery."

Sigfrid turns around in the middle of the parking lot.

"So have I." Her teeth shift upwards for a moment. "Do you think that newspaper report means anything?"

I shake my head in confusion, oh I don't know which way to look!

"Well I do. He wasn't a gold-miner for nothing. He hid his thousands down in the mine at Rossland."

Her eyes shine with such a dogmatic faith, there will be no denying her. She must believe in a fortune that cannot be found, and what can I believe in?

We come through the doors into the lobby, it is not the restaurant. Oh, the restaurant is down a long corridor to the left. We stand in front of the till, waiting for the hostess to seat us.

A dark girl with bobbed hair takes us to a table.

"Would you care for coffee?" she passes out the menus.

"Please," we all nod like children.

As soon as she goes away, Garney opens his menu. "I'm a hungry pilgrim," he concludes at once.

"What?"

Garney grins. "The Pilgrim breakfast. Two eggs, ham or bacon or sausage, two pancakes, toast, jelly, and all the coffee you can drink."

My eyes search the menu. He is right, the bowl of noodle soup we had last night in the hospital cafeteria wasn't much. The *Hungry Pilgrim* costs $2.75.

The waitress comes back with a stainless steel pot, Sigfrid holds her mug full under the black, plastic lid. My restlessness returns, I don't like to be served.

"Can I take your order?" she says when Garney's cup is filled.

Garney looks at me, I'm not ready. Sigfrid closes her menu.

"I'll have the pancakes without bacon," she looks shyly down at the table. Daddy used to make us pancakes when we were very little.

Garney waits again on me, I don't know what to do.

"I'll have the Pilgrim," he finally covers for my confusion. "Scrambled, please, with a slice of ham."

I glance up meekly.

"Toast and jelly, if it's not too much trouble."

Garney looks sideways at me as she writes briskly and then walks away.

"You pay for their trouble, that's why you come to a restaurant. When she comes back, I want you to order *breakfast*. You know how you are, you'll be the first to get the 'flu if you're run down."

"I'm not run down," I say quietly. "The sight of Daddy's digestion still bothers me, that's all."

Garney's nostrils widen and whiten at the thought. I should have found a better excuse.

"What do you think?" Sigfrid says abruptly, have I spoiled her breakfast too?

"Think about what?" Garney's voice is easy again, he is kindly inquiring.

"The Rossland Mine Museum. People said we should see it."

"We have to be at the funeral home at ten," I speak up gently. But Sigfrid's hope has got the best of her, she won't give up on Daddy till she's satisfied.

"It's only eight o'clock. The nurse said the funeral home doesn't open before ten."

I won't be satisfied with any outcome. Oh, I must try to be satisfied!

"You're not hoping," Garney smoothes out each word as if with kid gloves, "to locate your Dad's money in the mine, are you?"

The waitress comes back with our platters, the *Pilgrim* is as big as a boat! I suppose I wouldn't mind a tiny piece of ham and some egg.

"Chris?—" Garney looks curiously at me.

"No, thank you."

But he doesn't mean what I think.

"Would you mind a tour of the mine? If it doesn't seem disrespectful. . .?" He glances shyly at Sigfrid, he doesn't want her to think he is being critical.

"No, I wouldn't mind. But shouldn't we leave word at the hospital?"

"Well— Sigfrid is right about the time, we've got nearly two hours. And it's only five or six miles. Eight or ten kilometres, I mean."

He makes it so much easier for both of us, still we don't want to talk after such a decision. Each falls to her meal, digesting her thoughts.

"Well," Garney breaks the silence, laying his knife and fork to rest, "I'm one pilgrim who isn't hungry any more."

I drain the rest of my coffee, I will be ready when they are. The waitress with bobbed hair comes with the bill, it is $6.30. Oh, the toast and jelly was a dollar! Why didn't I have at least pancakes? Then I have to smile, it seems I can't be satisfied, no matter what!

Sigfrid takes her wallet out of her purse, Garney moves it away with one hand.

"I want to pay my own way," she says in a hurt voice.

He relents then, she counts out $2.25. "Is tax five per cent here?"

Garney nods in embarrassment, she gives him another dime and a nickel to be sure. He tucks her change with a dollar under his plate.

When we go outdoors, a light rain has swept in off the mountains, only the first three or four benches of homes are visible along the bottom of the mountain.

"I hope it's not like this," Garney looks at the sky with worried eyes, "in a couple of days when we go over the skyway to Creston."

He turns his headlights on before we drive out of the parking lot. It is now full day, our white car is like a rabbit against the snow.

At last we are leaving town. Almost at once, through the railway underpass, the sign says Village of Warfield. As we begin the steep climb out of the valley, the motor pulls so hard that Garney has to gear down. Sigfrid and I must be a nuisance crowding to see past him into the valleys. Still it is no use, the rain fills the void with shapes of cloud.

"There's the cemetery," Sigfrid says suddenly with her face turned away from me.

Oh, there it is, too, its snow-white terraces opening among the barren birches and dark evergreens like a blank page.

"I don't see any headstones," Sigfrid says again to the window.

I look up the hillside, we can't see to the rear of any terrace but the first one.

"I'm sure they have something," I try to reassure her. "Maybe the flat kind to fit in with the scenery."

She scowls, I hadn't expected her to be this way.

"I want a proper headstone for Daddy's grave, a white marble one with angels blowing horns at the corners."

Garney takes his eye off the road for just a moment, he looks expectantly at me.

"We don't have the money for something so elaborate, Sigfrid." It is true, there is always so much overhead in a store.

"Wouldn't it be better—" Garney's voice trails off lamely, he hates even to finish the thought.

"—to let him lie unnamed?" Sigfrid's bitterness leaves me feeling so hopeless. "I didn't think desertion was a crime in this day and age."

"I never said that," Garney appeals to me for help, I can't think what to say. "I don't know— I just thought it might be best not to make too— much—"

"Christine," Sigfrid's voice searches out the flaw in my own divided heart, "would you let Daddy go unremembered? Would you try to sweep his life under the carpet too?"

"I'm terribly sorry," Garney says at once. "I never meant it the way you took it."

I want to reach out and hold her, but something prevents me, oh I fear my mind would snap were I to deny my own truth right now. Still I cannot betray a one of us, there is no way left for me to turn!

132

Sigfrid sniffs the rest of the way up the mountain through the sleeting rain. None of us knows any more what to say to the others, we are a sorry lot when we grope past a damp wall of granite into sudden civilization. The flashing yellow light overhead directs us left onto Main Street. We go by intriguing old buildings without a second glance, listening to the grate of windshield wipers over glass. The rain has long since swirled into snowflakes. Now the whole town falls away to the left, we drive as on a razor's edge. A gap looms ahead in a ridge that was shadow; suddenly we are through and stopped at a T-intersection. The giant sign of the mine and its tower seem dwarfed by the beginnings of a mountain behind the curtain of snow.

"Whew, it's blowing like a prairie blizzard," Garney says, stopping the car in an empty parking lot. He turns up his jacket collar before he opens the door. I should have brought his heavy coat from Daddy's apartment.

Stiffly we climb the bank beneath a wooden tower. A monstrous engine sits behind a great flywheel, ropes like a giant's loom. But all stands idle behind the fence. Garney leads us in silence to the door of the museum.

"Good morning," a girl in a sweater and skirt waits behind a glass counter. "Do you want a tour of the museum and mine?"

"We'd like to see the mine," Sigfrid says determinedly, she doesn't look at either of us. Garney nods politely.

"It's the same fee for both. You might as well go see the museum while I ring for your guide at the mine."

Sigfrid shakes her head, she has her wallet out already.

"Take all three out of this," she holds out a $10 bill.

"No, Sigfrid," my voice sounds so breathless, "let us pay for you."

Garney is trying to reach the girl with a purple note too.

"I wouldn't think of it," Sigfrid says flatly. "You used your gas to come up here."

Garney looks hurt for a moment, then I see he means to take it, no matter the spirit of its giving.

"Thank you very much, Sigfrid," he says humbly.

And so our tongues are loosened once more, we have made a kind of peace without having to confess our differences.

"Did you know," Garney glances up from the pamphlet the girl has given him, "that this mine in 1901 introduced the eight-hour

133

working day to our weary old world? I should tell my boss about that."

"Tell me anything you like," I pretend to scowl, he appears to enjoy it as hugely as ever. Sigfrid laughs too. Oh I don't know what to hope for any more.

The guide breezes in with a gust of wind through the door.

"Oh," she gasps for breath, "that *is* wicked out there! Are you folks sure you want to climb so far?"

Garney grins, "Yes ma'am, we're from the prairies."

She gives him a freckled smile, "Why didn't you say so? Lovely day, isn't it?"

We all turn our collars up against the wind, Sigfrid follows our guide into the storm. We plod single-file up the icy steps behind the giant's loom. It is quiet among the trees, although the snow whirls madly overhead. Then we come out in a clearing where buckets hang like cable cars, the lines go right out of sight up the mountain. Now there is machinery everywhere, rusted tram cars and great gears and things.

Our guide stops to shout above the wind, "That building over there, we have to go over there." We scamper, with this wind at our tails, like a herd of mountain goats. Our guide bursts into the long, low house with the bunch of us at her heels. "Here," she points to a rack, "you might as well put on your hard hats right now."

Garney reaches for two yellow ones marked S, and an orange one marked L.

"If you'll follow me, I'll show you the rock room first," says our guide. "By the way, my name is Janet."

We give her our names too. Sigfrid says, "Our father used to be a lease miner here."

"Well," Janet says, "then you should have lots of questions."

But I miss most of the names of the rocks, including those that glow under violet light. Now I hesitate to ask, she might think I've got nothing upstairs! But Sigfrid will remember, I will ask her to tell Mother.

"We're going back outside, it's just a few yards to the tunnel," Janet says. "Watch you don't slip on the tramming tracks."

So away we go again, I wonder what Sigfrid expects to find, maybe a clue that only she would understand. We draw up at the mouth of a dark tunnel with lights running down the middle of the ceiling. I flinch at the sight of a bear on the hillside above the door, oh it is just a cut-out bear!

"This is Black Bear Portal," Janet follows my eyes. "Let's go inside."

The great timbers on either side of us are like the entrance to an ancient tomb I saw in one of Wayne's books. I feel drawn in spite of myself into these dim recesses. Before a great iron door, Janet stops.

"You see the Ingersoll-Rand drill? They called it the widow-maker, it raised so much stone dust that the drillers tended to die of silicosis."

As she undoes the latch of the great iron door, I feel my heart catch.

"This is the draft door, they kept it closed in summer to stop hot air from rushing in, and in winter to keep the warm air from getting out. Can you feel the draft?" A breeze is beginning to fan my cheek, if we leave the door open much longer it will take our breath away. Janet closes the door behind us, it clangs like the gate of a prison. Ahead on the narrow tracks there drips a puddle of water, I clutch at Garney's arm. He beams down at me, "Man, I'm glad we didn't miss this, aren't you?"

Oh I don't know how men could have spent their lives in here!

"All winter long," Janet seems to enter my thoughts, was I thinking out loud again? oh I must be careful! "the miners never saw the light of day. They would come to work in the dark and go home when the sun was down."

To lose the light...one might as well be lost oneself...given up for dead....Now the deeper we go, the more depressed I get, oh I don't want to delve into these depths any more!

We stop before a fork in the tunnels.

"This is the intersection with the Le Roi shaft," Janet says. "At this point you are standing three hundred feet beneath Red Mountain. There are two levels above us, at intervals of one hundred feet. The main shaft goes down fifteen levels beneath us."

Sigfrid's face blanches, it is apparent even in the dim light.

"Are we going to go to the bottom?"

Janet smiles. "You don't have to worry. Most of the mine is closed. There are pitfalls everywhere in the dark. Some of them drop six hundred feet. We just stay to the main road, so to speak."

Garney asks a question, but I am lost now in a maze without end.

I see we are come into a room with many timbers holding up the vault of stone. She is explaining about drifts, I look at the emptiness all about us.

Then we are in the hoist room, broken timbers and boards lie in a jumble on the floor like pick-up sticks. I could never take out the right one when I was a girl, but all would come tumbling. Sigfrid's face looks almost ghostly now in these shadows, I don't feel too well myself.

"You'll notice this stope," Janet brings us into another corridor, I would never find my way out of here again, "this is most likely where your father worked."

Together Sigfrid and I peer up at what seems to be a crypt in the wall.

"It's such a narrow slope," I say.

"Stope," Garney corrects me.

"How did men get inside it?" Sigfrid asks tremulously.

"It's really twenty inches wide, they had room enough to hold their drills up. They worked on ladders to a height of two hundred feet. The slope of the wall must have supported them some."

"Then there was a lot of gold brought out of this stope?" Sigfrid's voice, so unlike her, has an edge to it.

"Not much, I'm afraid, just enough to keep men like your father in hope of something better. I've heard my father say that the lease miners never found more than an ounce of gold in five tons of rock, and even then they had to share most of it with the smelter. They finally gave up hope in 1942, and the mine was closed down permanently."

Garney asks some more questions and reaches a little way into the crypt. I stand here like a silly old woman with nothing to say. I have come to the place where Daddy spent the better part of a man's life and I have nothing to offer, nothing more than he had to show for his labours. Sigfrid looks so hopelessly depressed, there is nothing I can say to help her. But strangely now I do not feel so depressed myself, there is something I don't understand taking place in my depths, a shifting sensation far beneath the surface.

We come toward the light of day at last, Janet has brought us safely through the maze of bulb-lit tunnels to the railhead of the tramming tracks. We walk out along the tiny rails to where snow swirls at the mouth of the cave. The tracks, I know, once led to the real railroad tracks and the line to the smelter down in Trail where even rock is melted away. After he gave up the hunt for gold, Daddy went to work there as a foreman, he was always so good with men.

"Thank you," I press Janet's hand as we stop before the curtain of snow. "Your tour has been a godsend." My tongue has framed the word before I know it, my mind still is not clear why exactly, but I feel it and I mean it.

"You've been a good audience," she replies warmly. "We always like to see alumnae of the mine and their children."

Sigfrid is sunk much too low to answer as she would if she were feeling better. Janet points our way back to the museum, oh she is going to stay up here by herself, she smiles and asks for our hard hats. *Nammen!* My eyes say we didn't mean to walk off with them. She smiles knowingly and, with a nod, trudges off in the direction of the rock room.

We descend through the peaceful fury of the storm. Snow flies too thick to make conversation necessary. Garney conducts us slowly, two aging sisters and an aging man, down the hill.

When we are back in the car and on our way out through town, he remarks softly, "He had a tough life, all right, that place made it come alive for me."

We don't answer, no reply is called for. We ride now in a world of snowy silence.

Beyond the shadow of the granite wall we turn downward, the valley lies unseen beneath us. Garney steers carefully, pumping the car on the treacherous slope, but it doesn't matter any more, one way or the other. There is no need to hope or not to hope, all is done that can be done.

Wayne

He paused when he heard the opening bars of *Solveig's Song*, then took his hand from the stereo dial. There wasn't even a hint of reproach in the mild phrases, violins singing only of faith and hope and sleep. More than anything, Karen needed to sleep.

He opened the French doors to the dining room. His wife sat so still, barely chewing her cereal, that he had to swallow a sudden lump in his throat. It had been weeks since she had enjoyed a good night's rest—ever since her mother lit into her again. And because she was so sensitive to light and sound, she couldn't even dream of a daytime nap.

He sat down, noticing a tiny flutter in her throat.

"Did you finally take a sleeping pill last night?"

The way she didn't hear him, he thought she might still be drugged. But her throat seemed to pulse with the harp-beat of the music. Perhaps it was helping. The violins took over again and he grew aware of a sound like a metronome. The clock-door, when he looked, was hanging wide open. They hadn't been able to fix it since the day it fell in the mounting and twisted both hinges.

Casually, so she wouldn't notice, he went to close it by way of the sideboard. He had some trouble clinching the nail Karen had driven into the fine cherry cabinet. Fortunately, the clockworks had not been affected; the weights kept their counterpoise halfway down the month.

Now her face was untroubled by the memory. Then, she had said fatalistically, "Maybe we should just chuck it. It's because of me, anyway, that it fell."

"Don't be silly," he had spoken kindly. "It's practically an heirloom. We can't just throw away the time we scraped to pay for it."

But when he had tried to close the door on the magnetic catch, the hinges sagged out of the wood.

"Heirlooms are for passing on," she went on in a half-abashed voice. "Why don't we just chuck it?"

"What was the point, then, of swiping the down payment from your sister?"

He couldn't deny that Connie and Bernie had cashed in by getting married right out of high school. The morning after the wedding, the presentations were stacked in neat piles of thousands in the front room of the Babiuk house. The floor, when he and Karen got up late, was littered with envelopes like unshredded confetti. Connie and Bernie had been back from the motel for hours, lusting where it really counted.

"*Boże*," Karen's Mom had said, "we should go back to the hall for the family lunch. Auntie Phyllis will be waiting, and Uncle Nick with his homebrew."

"Can't we finish up the tally first?" Bernie chuckled as if to make light of it, but his red eyes ferreted support without looking directly at anyone.

"I'm not going," Karen said quietly. "I have a headache."

Wayne took his cue from her. "I'm in pretty bad shape myself. I shouldn't have let Uncle Nick cut good rye with homebrew."

Bernie forced a grin, showing bad teeth.

"Don't you know what a headache means? You won't get a sniff."

"Quit your bragging, Bernie," Connie's dimples made a sweet smile all the sweeter. "Give other people a chance, eh?"

But Karen, when they did go back to bed, wasn't interested.

"I'm not like Connie. I can't do it under Mom's nose."

"That's not what you said before we were married."

"Then you shouldn't have married me." She sat up and snatched

139

her housecoat from the card table, stepping into it briskly.

"Come back to bed. I'll let you sleep, I promise."

"I'm up. I don't feel like lying down now."

He sagged for a quarter hour, listening to the swish of blood behind his eardrums. There was a stealthy sound of ripping in the front room.

The sliding door squealed a little as he slipped in sideways. Karen started up from her chair.

"What are you doing?"

"Just helping Connie a little." She kept her head bowed. "I might as well do something if I'm not going to clean up the hall." Then she looked over her shoulder at him so innocently that he became flustered.

"Look, I didn't mean— Karen, I'm sorry about what happened in the bedroom."

She bowed her head again. The sight of the exposed knuckles on her spine touched him with pity. He stooped, gripping her in a clumsy bear hug. But when he tried to kiss her cheek, she tucked her chin into her bosom. Too far, as it turned out. He heard something crackle.

"What are you hiding?" he said tonelessly.

"Nobody gave us any money when we got married."

"Karen, you didn't!"

When she wouldn't deny it, he could only say helplessly, "How much?"

"Connie got what people would have presented to me."

"How much, Karen?"

She hung her head.

"Twenty dollars."

"Well," he shrugged, "if a few crumbs is all it takes—"

But he couldn't deny her. Not when it was for his sake she had given up a Ukrainian wedding. His folks would have stayed home, it was as simple as that.

Solveig's Song was measuring out its peaceful close: a phrase of violins repeated on the woodwinds; deep assent from the bass; then full and lasting harmony.

Karen appeared soothed by it. Her face, almost sour and slovenly at times, had opened like a pale pink rose, propped in the cup of her hand. The image of her sitting with her elbow on the table brought a rush of tenderness for her, for the only tender image she had salvaged

140

from a terrible childhood. Still her mother had always turned it around, making it sound like an accusation. "*Oy Boże*, you were all the time so tired, Karen, when you were little. You used to fall asleep with your chin in your hand at supper."

Yet Karen sat before him as that curable child, so tired out from play she might even sleep bolt upright at the table. He reached for her blue-veined wrist and stroked it. Miraculously her face had kept its light, almost a nimbus that outshone the dark circles under her eyes. He loved her even more for the way pain had made her beautiful.

"It'll be okay," he sought the dreaming child who found a future after all. "You'll come through it like you always do."

But she rolled her eyes without turning her face toward him.

"There's only one sure way to sleep," she said dully. "I hate being noble at breakfast."

"Sorry." Then, after a moment, "You really shouldn't use that word *hate*, you know. You'll end by hating your life."

She only looked at him out of the corner of one eye.

He couldn't help thinking of her *Baba* going crazy in the flat behind the old poolroom in town. Karen had joked once or twice how it would be an ideal place to live—just two doors down from his parents' store.

He tried to chew a mouthful of cereal. The box proclaimed it *la céréale que Mikey aime!* But the sight of the kid's freckled face on the box made him shiver a little   *here for Baldr   the mead is brewed   the shining drink*   She couldn't have meant what she said about   *a shield lies o'er it*   one sure way to sleep   *but their hope is gone   from the mighty gods*   and then he couldn't stop a shudder from taking him violently   *unwilling I spake*   life at any cost, even a life of pain   *I spake   and now would be still*

"Why do you want to go home anyway?" he reasoned without much hope. "Why beggar yourself? She's not going to give you her Good Housekeeping Seal of Approval."

The muscle in her throat fluttered like a tiny lung. It was the only sign he had sometimes that she was still listening. Abruptly she lowered her chin and squeezed her eyes tight, shaking her head to hold back the tears.

And then he saw her as he first had done that night ten years ago. She had met him in the side landing to the boxy little house beside her father's HiWay garage down in SkiTown.

"Come in and meet my Mom," she had said hopefully. A cold sore, like a scab, had broken out on her lip. The night before, when they had met on a ride out from Saskatoon, she had been without blemish.

He followed her up from the landing, already smelling a kitchen as sour and dark as the varnished wainscotting. His eyes lighted on the carved roast of pork, fouled with grease and garlic, sitting in an open roaster on the stove.

"Mom," Karen spoke into the darkened breakfast nook, "this is my date, Wayne Goodman."

The woman chuckled.

"Hello, Mrs Babiuk," Wayne sought her face where it loomed, round and coarse and red, out of the shadows. His father had told him to study the mother's face if he wanted to see the daughter twenty years from now.

"Wayne is from Lacjardin, Mom. From the store next to your old place."

Mrs Babiuk chuckled again. Her bulging cheekbones gave her a popeyed expression. Suddenly she beamed on him, speaking to her daughter without looking at her.

"He's too good for you."

Then the vein had fluttered in Karen's throat and Wayne's eyes flicked back to the mother's head bristling like a pot scrub. The old lady bore no resemblance to the daughter. He felt half in love with the girl already, and totally helpless to save her from that face as remorseless as fate.

But hadn't her father proved that escape was possible—if only he had put his mind to it? Metro had come to stay with them soon after they were married, hoping to find a job and a new life for himself in Saskatoon. "This time," he set a nine of hearts on Wayne's 15-2, making a run of three, "I'm not going back. Mom never likes my plans anyways. Everything I do is wrong." His slope shoulders lifted a little. "Let her yell, for all I care. She can yell at an empty house if she wants."

"So things have been bad again?" Wayne wished he could help.

Metro shrugged. But his hand shook while he chain-lit a cigarette.

"Last week the drain was plugged in the kitchen sink. Mom blamed it on me for rinsing my teeth. But sometimes I get raspberry seeds stuck under my plate, I have to get them out. 'I don't rinse them in the kitchen,' I said. But she wouldn't hear nothing how the kitchen and bathroom had different pipes."

He paused such a long time that Wayne had to ask, "Is that all?"

Metro looked at him without any expression, his eyes flat as water. Perhaps he mistook silence for suspense. Finally he shrugged.

"I watched her one time after supper. She was scraping the mashed potatoes and wege-tables into the sink. 'The pipe gets stopped up with all that garbage,' I said. The plate she was holding come flying like a frisbee. That's how I got this mark above my eye. I didn't have no time to think about tracking my blood around, she was yelling and throwing everything she could get her hands on."

"Good god! What did you do?"

Metro's lips were no more pouty than usual. But his eyes were red and moist. "She made me clean up after she went to wisit Mrs Klimchuk."

The next day Wayne heard him in the kitchen telling the story over again. At the end he said, "Don't let on to Mom I told you nothing."

"Why not, Metro?" Wayne called. "You're not going back to her, are you?"

He strode into the kitchen when Metro didn't answer.

"Well, are you?"

"Could be." Metro wouldn't look at him.

"But that's the most hopeless goddamn atti—"

Karen shook her head and suddenly it was clear that Metro wanted to go back. There was nothing else to talk about with his fund of stories spent.

Metro did sit around the basement apartment several more days, smoking till the curtains reeked. The day Karen told him so much smoking couldn't be good for his heart, he took the bus back to Nisooskan.

"Give me one good reason for going home," Wayne dared Karen to do better. "Tell me what you can hope for without being ground under again."

She shook her head like a person refusing news of bereavement.

"Karen," he pleaded, "why should you care what she thinks any more? She's only envious because you're not like her. Connie's her girl, don't you know, all mush and gush about mothers? That's your problem too, if you'd only admit it. You just want a different one. Write it off as childish nonsense. And then you're homefree."

143

"I can't be like you."

"Why not?"

"Oh, forget it."

"Why don't you say what you mean?"

"Some things," she took a long swallow of coffee, "should be obvious."

"You mean my grandfather, don't you? Well, I'm not going to meet him in case I turn out to be like him."

Her stare withered his ready grin. Then he wished he could be more like his own father, laughing things off. Even that twenty-five pounds he was supposed to lose.

"Thank you," Garney had said the other night when Karen offered him some baking with his coffee, "I really shouldn't. Is that lemon loaf? Lemons neutralize calories, don't they? Maybe just one, then." But when he had to get up a third time to help himself, he joked, "I haven't had more than my eighteen hundred calories— tonight. Neither of you is going to tell Mom, I hope?"

He was still too much of a gentleman to bring up the subject of Mom's bus ride to Trail with Auntie Sigfrid. More precisely, he wasn't going to blame Wayne for not chaperoning them in the family car. Even when Karen had first gone out of the room to get lunch, he had steered around the topic.

"Man," he smiled, "I thought I was going to have my car bilingual before I made this trip. But the stupid thing hasn't learned a word of metric."

"You don't have to drive to beat sixty." Wayne saw the opening, then gave it anyway. "Just don't let Big Foot take the wheel."

"You wouldn't— I don't suppose you could get off, eh?" For a split second he looked naked without his grin. Then he looked down in mock concern at his broad foot. "It's lonely keeping company with clodhoppers."

"Not half as lonely as it's going to be in a crowd of Norwegians."

"Now you're talking my language," Garney smiled broadly.

"Mom will translate for you," Wayne tried to hide his bitterness. "Hasn't she spent a lifetime translating black into white?"

"I bane tinking a lot," Garney's eyes weren't smiling like his lips. "I vil snakker yust *norsk*. Den maybe I vil *lusa* veight."

"Dad, I'm sorry. I don't know. I'm sorry, I guess, that I can't go with you. But I really don't want to set eyes on the old bugger. Not after what he's done to Mom."

144

"She's ready to forgive and forget, son." The mask was off now, his Dad's lips as grave as his eyes.

"Yeah? She was ready the day he ran off fifty years ago. She's denied her whole life because of him. Maybe you don't see it, you're her husband. But she's always wanted her kids to be just like her."

"Your sister wishes she could come. But somebody has to stay home to mind the store."

"How does that disprove my point? Dad, don't take this personally. But you always—well, you went along with her. I'm not going to help her any more to make up for his life. It's time somebody said no to her."

"You've been saying no to her," Garney was joking again, "since the day she set you in the highchair. Do you remember? You used to make her gobble half your food before you'd even taste it."

But Wayne couldn't joke. "Are you saying that's why she went ahead to Trail?"

His father's grin had little in common with his shrewd eyes.

"You have no idea how many times I've used that trick on her. My only trouble, usually, is to make her think I need what she's scared to take for herself."

The storekeeper's mask was in place again, and the chance for revelation was passed.

But the trouble with Karen now was not that she'd seen through Wayne's mask; the trouble, as always with her, was saving any face at all.

"Okay," he faked a grin, "so I'm not supposed to joke." But when she still looked right through him, he blurted, "What am I supposed to be? Grand-paw's spitting image?"

Sometimes the way his mother looked at him .... Then mercifully the image of his father's rotund face came up like a shield. Surely his own puss had a hint of that same roundness. He knew his hair was just as lank and loose as his Dad's. If only he had been a chunky kid, instead of a skinny scion ....

"I can't pretend," Karen said coolly, "that I have no family. Not even your grandfather pretends that any more."

"Do you really think it would do me much good to bow down to him? Are you happy being your mother's creature?"

She ignored the belated question.

"It's probably your last chance to catch him at his worst."

145

"If you mean—"

"I only mean," she backed off quickly, "that we all have skeletons in the family closet. It wouldn't hurt you to look at your own for a change."

"I see." They were both silent for a time. "It doesn't matter that I want to write about them, I suppose. You want me to go wallow in them."

"I didn't say *wallow*, did I? But you know how much your mother wanted you to be reconciled with him."

"I've still got classes to teach."

"That's just an excuse. It's not like you grew up under his influence, you know. He doesn't have to be your fate."

"But your mother does, I suppose?"

"If you were really as free, Wayne, as you let on, you wouldn't be scared shitless to see him."

"And I wouldn't be free, either, to imagine him. That's the only way I know, Karen, to be rid of him. To tell his story."

"Hide behind it, you mean."

But as soon as she saw the look on his face, she relented.

"Alright, since you're so free, you be the one to lead us into the future. I don't see why I should have to make all the calls to the adoption agency."

"Fine." He was glad to change the subject. "Just as long as you don't go and change your mind again."

The pendulum clock whirred, striking in the empty silence.

Karen sprang from the table with dirty dishes in hand.

"I'm going to miss the bus if I don't get going."

"Leave that stuff," Wayne ordered. "I'll clean up when I get home. I've only got one class this morning anyway."

"Thanks." She hurried toward the stairs.

"You're sure you won't change your mind about going?"

"Wayne!" she turned at the door, sounding hurt, "you know Mom is expecting me."

146

The sidewalk was covered with a light blanket of snow. He opened the squealing garage door and sidled alongside the car. He pumped the footfeed four times, then turned the key. It started easily, plugged in all night. He got the snowshovel down and went out to scrape the walk.

When the letter had come Monday, Karen had sagged at the sight of her mother's handwriting. She had begun to come up a little from Christmas, too, from telling her mother she could return those ceramic canisters. Yes, she bloody well had warned her not to get them! She didn't care if they *were* nice Ukrainian designs on them, the point was that she had *so* told her they would be wasted inside a cupboard.

"I liked them so much when I saw them," the old lady blustered, "I thought you would appreciate them. But you're fussy. You must be rich. Anything I ever got, I never said nothing. I said it was okay."

"Mom, they're very nice. But what good are they if I don't have room for them in my kitchen? I wish just once you'd think of what I want. Or spend your money on something I could use."

"Next time you won't get no more gifts."

That was Boxing Day. Karen had fought her depression for more than two weeks before the letter came.

"When you talked to me like that," the old lady wrote, "I was sick. You are young. I am old and my nerves can't take bad problems no more."

"Oh, get off it," Wayne had said when he read it. "She's been saying the same damn thing ever since I've known her."

"She *is* old," Karen said wearily. "I shouldn't have said anything. I've got to make it up to her somehow."

He was cleaning the bottom step when Karen came out on the high back stoop. Just the sight of her white face against the blank stucco hurt him.

"Here," he hurried to take the suitcase and overnight bag from her while she locked the house.

He backed their eight-year-old Mustang out of the garage before she slipped into her bucket seat beside him.

"It really hurts me," he said as he swerved in the deep ruts of the back alley, "to see you go running every time she squawks. You're not responsible for her misery, you know. You deserve a little happiness yourself."

147

She rode in silence. He had to look away to check the traffic from Five Corners.

"Do you realize how tired you've been since her letter came? You've been going down as fast as a leaky balloon."

"It's not all her fault."

He looked across at her in surprise.

"Wayne, I've got to do something with my life. Ever since we came back from Winnipeg, I've been typing your thesis, and now the revisions to make it a book. Maybe it's time I did something for myself."

"Weren't you glad, though, not to teach any more? Or do you want to go back to school, is that it?"

"I don't know. Sometimes it feels like life is passing me by. Maybe I won't change my mind this time if we apply for adoption."

He strained to lift his foot off the accelerator. The car slewed on a patch of ice.

Charlie's silent little head looked plucked. Why had Mom clipped his hair so high like that? Straight as a shingle above his ear before the grey stuff oozed— Charlie wouldn't answer now. Where was Charlie gone?

Dad stayed in the car with them while Mom climbed the wooden steps to *Mor's* house. Kerestin held little Elizabeth in her arms like a real Mom. Wayne leaned over the front seat to ask Dad if he knew where Charlie had gone. But the tears were splashing off his father's chin like rain from overflowing eaves. Then he was terrified to think that Dad might not hear him either. Not ever again.

"You're driving too fast."

He pumped the brakes in time to his heart. The light at the bottom of the bridge had turned green, letting the flow of traffic come at him. He crowded into the righthand lane, forgetting to signal. A horn blared so close behind him that he had to fight another skid.

"Do you think it's a good idea, though," he said when he had exited safely onto Fourth Avenue, "to mix up a child in our unsolved problems?"

She looked at him intently.

"What I mean is, it's hard to consider being a father until I do something about my grandfather."

"Go face him, then."

"Is facing your mother going to solve anything this weekend?"

She hesitated. "I'm not the only one who's got a mother problem, you know."

The thought of all he had put up with—her sorrows he had borne, the privations he had suffered, the understanding he had afforded her endlessly repeated story—it angered him to be reduced to the same level.

"I didn't have one before I met you."

"That's not fair, Wayne, and you know it. Your mother loves me like a daughter. She's the closest thing I've ever known to a real mother."

"For god's sake, look at yourself, Karen. You're still hoping. You know what a peril they are, even when they mean well. If I can give up a mother, why can't you?"

"I told you before. I'm not like you."

"Yes, I know. You Ukrainians have loose morals. Just like Mother said when her son was going to marry one."

Karen flushed a little and he could tell, by her downcast eyes, that he had brought back the whole business with Nestor. He hadn't meant to . . . . Even after seven years of marriage, it still hurt. Nestor had been her fiancé, so it was none of his business, really. Still she had wanted to tell him everything in his father's car that night, so shy she couldn't spell it out at first, so honest she wouldn't try to spare herself.

"It doesn't matter," he had raised her lowered chin with the tips of his fingers. "I love you now."

She raised incredulous eyes, seeking a flicker of doubt, till at last he saw tears start to her lashes. Still she held back.

"Mom was right. You *are* too good for me."

"That's bullshit. Nobody should be a virgin at twenty any more."

"Nestor didn't believe me the first time," her mind skipped tracks like a phonograph needle. "He wouldn't take my word for it that it was an operation that took away—you know."

149

"Don't worry about the bastard. He's history."

"Oh Wayne, I'm so sorry."

He had to say quite firmly at last, "No, I don't want it to be because of him. Not the first time."

Nestor had gotten laid wherever he could and then arranged to double his pleasure by having Karen find out.

"You're sure," Wayne said suddenly, "that you don't *want* your mother to hurt you?"

"Don't worry about my mother," she stared straight ahead, "until you've come to terms with yours."

"You don't have to worry about her any more."

"I know. She's not the one who thinks you're better than me."

"Be reasonable, Karen."

"I am being reasonable. After seven years, don't you think I can see? I'm finished taking the blame all the time."

She sat so still, her face so sallow with the rising sun behind them, that he couldn't be angry.

"If you like," he said finally, "I'll call Child Care today."

He had to stop for some chilly pedestrians in the crosswalk by the Bus Depot. He looked hopefully in her direction. Her lips were pressed tightly together; she seemed blanched.

"How about it? Do you still want to have a baby with me?"

"I wouldn't have a pet with you."

Then she was out the door and gone before he knew what was happening. He watched the sway of her hips through the long, suede coat and for an instant he wanted to run up behind that eyeless insolence and make it aware of him. He considered driving off with her luggage. She would either miss her bus or be forced to visit her mother without a change of underwear.

Reluctantly he got out of the car and fished the suitcases out of the trunk. It goaded him to have to follow so meekly. She used to pull these stunts every other week, before she learned to be civilized. Once, before they were married, there had been that squabble at Pike Lake ... probably about sex. Everything in those days was about sex, the closer they got to the altar. Then, in front of hundreds of people, she had said, "Why don't you just fuck off?" And stalked off toward the car, leaving him to follow. The hard-packed sand on the beach had refused to swallow him up.

Now the sun on the snow made his eyes go dim. He could barely see it glint on the glass doors of the Bus Depot. Karen had vanished.

He shifted both cases into one hand, getting ready to yank the door open. They were his only dowry, these cheap pieces of luggage from an oil company promotion at her father's garage   *turn in at the sign of the big B/A   where motor products lead the way*   The melody veered, becoming the tune to a pop song played by every radio station in town   *Hop on the bus, Gus   You don't need to discuss much   Just drop off the key, Lee   And get yourself free*

The rush of warm air in the vestibule took his breath away. For a moment he saw the provincial coats of arms flutter overhead. Then he had to face a host of bearded men, huge vikings resting elbows and fists on shield and axe round the great hall. He blinked to get the sunspots out of his eyes. It was steadying to see only the usual sort of people—pensioners, Indians, young mothers—waiting on the moulded orange chairs.

Karen had her back to him at the ticket counter, taking money out of her purse. He waited, feeling anger turn, then love flow back like a tide.

She turned, head half-bowed, touching him with pity...but the clench of her jaw was her damn mother all over again.

"Maybe I should ask you first," her eyes didn't waver, "before I pay for a one-way ticket. Will you go to see your grandfather or not?"

He set her suitcases down smartly and walked off. Still he paused at the door, thinking of the sway of her hips...on a crowded beach. He bolted.

But he was watching out his rear window when the red-and-yellow bus nosed into the street. The tinted glass and glare of distant sun made it impossible to tell if she was watching for him. Then the STC logo on the side turned away from him. He was pulled out of the car by a fading hope that she wouldn't have gone without a word. The air smote his cheeks like the flat of an axe. He strode through the squeaking snow around the building and into the empty bus bays, but her luggage was gone from the middle of the floor.

He remembered waking in his own mother's house with his luggage unpacked in the middle of the room. Last year's mementos on the walls seemed like the belongings of a stranger...yellowed clippings of the 'Rider's Grey Cup...ranks of blue uniforms on the

Leafs' calendar pinched from his Dad's store...emblems of another life where all you did was watch....

While he stood noisily above the toilet, the silence of the house was like a reproach.

"Wayne?" he heard his mother's quiet voice as he passed in the hall. He looked into her bedroom, startled to find her lying down in the middle of the day.

"Mom, are you sick?"

"I'm just a little tired."

"I'm sorry if I woke you coming in last night."

She rolled her head slightly on the pillow.

"Your father," her lower lip began to quiver, "found a pair of panties in our car this morning."

His face was an open book where Karen's words might be read: "What the hell, don't worry about them. Next time I won't wear any. You'll only try to get them off."

"You're sure they're not someone else's," he blurted.

"Kerestin wouldn't let a boy do a thing like that...."

Two great tears were sliding down her freckled cheeks.

She had not always been mid-Victorian. Not that one time, anyway, when his father peeped at her in the bath, then flung the door wide for all his kids to see. She was caught standing angelically...her skin rosy and shining...her eyes proud, before she covered her breasts demurely with her elbows. "Garney!" she half laughed, half protested, "not in front of the children!"

"What did Dad say?"

"He doesn't want you to use his car any more. Not if you're going to bring public shame on us."

"Mom!"

"Right in the open," she barely breathed, "where anyone could see. Beasts in the field...those Ukrainian people...they're not like us. You don't know. The filthy women Daddy went to—"

He stared at her in amazement. Her father's life had been tabu with her, she would never speak about it....

She covered her face with her hands.

Then he was crying with her, denying his very manhood.

Karen wept too when he told her, looking away to blow her nose before she faced him.

"What will you do?" her voice was hard like her mother's.

152

He looked at the tiny brown curls tufting out of her bikini bottoms, then at the tops of her breasts in their red halter.

"I don't know," he said truthfully. "Maybe we should try not to see each other for awhile."

He watched her walk away on the wet, packed sand. Her feet left no mark behind. His eyes settled on the natural sway of her hips till he lost sight of them in the shade of the poplars where her roommate's car was parked.

After a time, he began to look for a familiar face on the beach. It wasn't that far back to the city. Before too long the traffic would be steady.

But a couple of days later he couldn't believe how much he still suffered. He found himself loitering on the driveway of the shabby rooming house on Osler Street where he and Karen had met in the winter. He walked off quickly, trying to put the past behind him.

On campus the greystone walls looked more beautiful than ever with the blush of evening sun on them. Karen used to meet him on the path by the Bowl, coming from Education to have lunch with him in Marquis Hall. He stopped on the marble steps of the library, fighting his need to tour the carrells. Too many students would be necking their way through Summer School. He broke and went inside to a payphone.

Karen's telephone rang as if in a different universe.

He loitered under the trees in the courtyard of two residence halls. He tried not to look at the couples strolling hand in hand through the doorways.

He called again on the hour. No answer.

Back in his wretched cubby-hole, he undressed and lay naked on the bed. The waterpipes groaned in the bathroom below. There was the murmur of a voice on the telephone in the room across the hall. He plumped the black box on his belly and dialled again. His pulse doubled the ringing in his ear. Wasn't it a sign of weak character that she couldn't stay home even one night?

At least the beer parlours would kick them out soon. He imagined her stupid with drink.

At one o'clock, the ringing ended with a grateful click.

"It's about time," he said before she could speak.

"Who is this?" her roommate said with a yeasty gush.

"Lisa, put Karen on, for crying out loud."

153

"Wayne?" She sounded fuddled. "Karen's—out."

It was so hot as he hurried down the Twenty-fifth Street bridge that the breeze off the river didn't cool him. The lamp poles swarmed with bugs as furious as thoughts. He had no plan, no hope other than to put himself in her way at the door. Couldn't she imagine a man changing his mind?

Fifth Avenue was a deep canyon of trees where streetlights shone remote as stars. He looked into parked cars as he strode along, then back at the row of screened verandas. There were no cars, thank god, in front of Karen's house.

Farther up the street something moved...a pair of legs waving in a car window. His pants stretched with the rush of blood. Maybe it wouldn't hurt to take in the sights before she came home. And here his mother thought it was only Ukrainians....

Bare heels drummed on the upholstered roof of the sporty red Monza. A pair of legs in jeans bent up the side of the window. Then he could see the guy's ass driving like a piston, the girl's legs sawing on his ribs like she would go through the roof. He craned to get a better view of her transported face, turned sideways against the far wall.

He hit the roof with his fist.

"Karen!"

She was half-sitting up, looking at him with shame and fear and pity. The guy, whoever it was, was having trouble untangling his long legs. Karen pushed his chest away with one hand, shaking her head slightly, unable yet to move, or even to pull down her skirt.

Then the car door opened. He looked away, waiting for the welcome squeal of tires. Her drunken voice was like a caress upon a bruise.

"Wayne? You might as well meet Nestor Kischuk."

At least she stood fully dressed, only her skirt so badly creased at the bottom.

"How can you be so fucking civilized—so to speak?"

"Nobody asked you to watch."

Nestor was still unfolding himself like a long cutout doll. Then he towered over them, a self-satisfied smile on his valentine face.

"Nestor Kischuk, Wayne Goodman. Nestor and I go ba-ack," she hiccuped slightly, "a long way."

154

The oaf flung one loose arm over Karen's shoulder, looking down at Wayne. She shrugged him off, leaving him to rock unsteadily.

"Why?" Wayne knew he reeked of self-pity. "Why would you go back to this bozo?"

The clown had the nerve to smile!

The jolt of his fist on that pointed chin hurt Wayne clear to his shoulder. The bugger didn't even go down, but grinned, daring him to do his worst. The moment he drove his fist up from his belt, something like a two-by-four clubbed him on the side of the head....

You do see stars he was thinking when he came to with his head in a soft lap. They were somewhere inside a porch. Karen's verandah. He recognized the wicker chair in the corner.

"How did I get here?" he said, before he heard her crying softly. She cradled his head.

"We carried you."

"May I ask if he's gone?"

"If you want him to be."

"I want you, Karen. I want you to be mine."

She gave him a kiss that must have put a crick in her neck. Now even the soft pressure of her breast made his head hurt.

"Where?" she paused for breath.

"Lisa's pissed to the gills. She wouldn't hear a thing."

"Do you mean in the same room?"

"I don't care who sees." In a cracked, defiant voice, he heard himself say, "We're getting married anyway."

"At first glance," he tried to remember something beyond the rushing bus which carried his wife away, "*Baldrs draumar* looks like a tightly knit poem. But because of one apparent flaw...." Hadn't she ever stopped to consider how dangerous it was for him to look his demon in the eye? "...most scholars think *Baldr's Dreams* is a late imitation of *The Lay of Thrym.*"

He stopped to scan the dozen faces in the classroom. Get on with it, they said. Spare us the learned introductions.

"You remember the situation. The Thing has been convened to find a cause for Baldr's terrible dreams. Othin leaves to ride down to

Hel. The wise-woman he's raised from the dead doesn't want to answer his questions. But he presses her to answer *'till all he knows.'* Finally she recognizes him, and they exchange parting insults. Now where's the flaw in that little scheme?"

The honey-blonde in the front row sat up. More often than not, she wore short skirts and crossed and uncrossed those dazzling thighs.

"I'd say the flaw is Odin's bad manners. I mean, here she is waking up from the dead to answer his questions and all he can give her for thanks is scorn."

Wayne looked into those steady green eyes and stepped forward.

"So you think, Sheila, that the poem doesn't account for his bad behaviour?"

"No, I don't. The *Völva* herself protests that he made her travel a *'fearful road.'* When she asks him just who he thinks he is, he gives her a false name, then dumps on her as soon as he's got what he wanted. I don't think it's called for. He's a jerk."

The general shout of laughter drove off his cares for the moment.

"You may not be too wide of the mark," he said with a grin. "Don't forget a handy theory, though, that we looked at a few weeks ago. You remember? The one about insults and riddles in the *Eddic* songs? Othin's personal habit of deceit and scorn might still have some social analogues today. Scholars have compared it to the practice of mumming in Newfoundland. Does anybody remember the connection?"

A hand waved three rows back. Murray's pale brow was scored like a palimpsest. Wayne could always count on him to understand the implications of what he'd heard.

"Isn't it in the way mummers also come in disguise and deceive their hosts? So long as no one knows who they are, respectable people can say really smutty things. And women can show aggression to men. It's a way of letting out frustrations. Or maybe even breaking the shell of convention."

"Good," Wayne started to say when Sheila broke in.

"I don't think a god has to take his frustrations out on a woman. I mean, he's the authority. She's the one who could better stand to have things reversed for awhile."

Every eye was on him, waiting for his answer.

"She can't be an ordinary woman, though, can she? Not if, like he says, she's the mother of three giants."

"Yeah, sure, but he's only telling her she's a dummy because the wise-women all have to be virgins."

"Have we really established that the insult-stanza is the problem?"

"Isn't it the previous one?" Murray ventured after a generally hostile silence. "Othin's last question seems almost irrelevant: *'Who are the maidens   who shall weep   and toss to the sky their neckerchiefs?'* What's that got to do with his other three questions: For whom are the benches of Hel decked out? Who's going to slay Baldr? Who's going to avenge him? Doesn't tossing neckerchiefs around look trivial by comparison?"

"Unless *hálsa scautom* is a kenning for chins."

"How do you throw chins up to heaven?" Sheila said witheringly.

"I guess the only possible way would be to dance ecstatically. Fleck says, in fact, that Othin is asking the *Völva* which girls will cry during Baldr's funeral and throw up their chins, or rather, who will do the ecstatic dance of death and die with him?"

"So why—" Then Murray's face shone like the rising moon. "Oh, I get it. He's not even looking for an answer now. He's just showing her, like he did the giant Vafthruthnir, who he is. It's another epiphany of Othin."

"Exactly."

But Sheila's eyes were still troubled.

"You don't think so, Sheila?"

"I don't see why, if he was only showing off again, he wouldn't say what he did to Vafthruthnir: *'What did Odin whisper in the ear of his son   before they laid Baldr   on the bale-fire?'* It would be just like him to win her head too by asking something that only he could know about."

Murray's eyes danced with joy.

"It's because Baldr isn't dead yet!"

"That's a more probable answer, I think," Wayne tried not to be partial. "The poet has to invent some way for Othin to reveal himself in this unusual chronology. And he has to do it within the usual brief space, so he can only do it by implication. But in effect he asks, 'Which girls will be ready to be buried with Baldr?' "

"Isn't that just what I've been saying all along?" Sheila sat up indignantly. "The gods of the Vikings are only looking for scapegoats."

But even as she stared at him, he saw her resentment turn to concern.

"Professor Goodman? Are you alright?"

He had heard a woman weeping just as Karen floated into the church on a flood of sunshine. She paused, checking her train, then tightened her hold on her father's arm. Her face behind the veil was as bright as the glory in which she stood. And yet the storm of lamentation threatened to break with the pealing organ, break and wash them all away.

His eyes darted over the sea of faces, focussing on his mother in the second pew to his right. Her face looked like a crumpled rag beneath the broad, green brim of hat. She gripped the pew-back, her knuckles white as her chin, eyes screwed tight, barely able to hold back until the first bars of "Here Comes the Bride" had turned every head. Then her chin came up as if she were howling and Wayne didn't know where to look, he couldn't face Karen yet, though he could see the hem of her gown advance like drifting snow.

The day Charlie died his mother had sat in the street with the body in her lap, not making any sound, not even stroking the little cheek, but only Wayne's where it touched cooling flesh. Neither did she burst into tears when they left the hospital, pausing at the head of the steep stairs for a moment, then climbing carefully down. Not even in the same pew where she now made such a fuss did she break that terrible silence. Only when the first spade of dirt broke over the lid of the casket did she cry out. And then her knees gave right away; his father had to hold her up lest she fall into the hole.

"Mama!" he had cried, terrified to find himself shut out of her pain, more frightened still to think she wanted to be buried with her baby.

Now as his bride paced near, his mother cried the same way for him, as if the dirt were closing over his head. Karen's eye, through the misty veil, caught his eye. She smiled. His own smile was forced. And then, together, they turned to face the minister. His mother's sobbing fell off a little, then died altogether.

158

He had been so afraid, before Charlie was born, that the birth would kill her. He had hated his father for the carelessness, even the obscene selfishness, that now threatened her. Till she came home from the hospital, glowing with love, and the fair-haired little babe had stolen all their hearts away.

Yet his mother never doubted that both her boys were stolen from her, Wayne as much as Charles, by the curse of her father's life. He had never forgiven her those tears, the feeling he had died in her eyes. Let her go and be buried, if she wished, drawn down by the old boy into his grave.

Sheila's eyes brimmed with concern. "Professor Goodman? Are you alright?"

He had not been right to let her stand in his stead. It was his mother's love, not her sacrifice, that must be suffered. Shame made him dizzy, as if the floor were opening all around him. He could only hope that the old boy was still kicking, that he might get there in time.

He was still quite dizzy when he let himself in at the back door of the house. He waited for his eyes to adjust after the blinding glare of sunlight on snow. The hollow tick of the clock echoed through empty rooms. He was too tired to climb the stairs from the landing. Then he heard a stirring in the living room.

"Karen?" His heart leaped. But there was no answer. His pulse quickened when he remembered there had been several break-ins this month along the street. He thought fleetingly of going out to call the police. But why should he? What was the use of catching them red-handed?

After a time his curiosity got the better of him and he tiptoed out through the kitchen. The rustling sound went on with a strange regularity.

He put a hand on the doorpost, peeping in. No one. He took a full step in before the swish sounded again. He glanced into the shadows by the rubber plant. Under the ten-foot ceiling, there was a man hanging and twisting by his bare heels! He was stark naked. As if he sensed Wayne's presence, he arched, then writhed around. Wayne felt his heart thud like an axe against a leather shield. Blood spilled from an ugly gash in the man's side, streaming over his throat and his terrible choked face. The head jerked, then fixed him with one closed eye. It was a moment before Wayne realized what was looking right through him was a muscle, like a squirming oyster, in the bloody socket. A loud shriek contorted those agonized lips, before it ripped from his own throat as well.

Mr. Batchelar was a small, grave man. He presided over a small teapot, quite as ill at ease with his hands as he appeared to be in his ill-fitting blue suit. His hair was combed in wisps, shedding flakes of dandruff onto padded shoulders.

"It should be ready," he looked anxiously at the teapot. "How do you like it, Mr Goodman? With sugar? Lemon, maybe? I'm afraid I don't have fresh lemon—"

"Straight is fine," Wayne said in a shaken voice. Karen had not sounded surprised at first when he called. He could hear her mother's voice in the background, pushing like a garlic press.

"Just the way it is, thanks," he said to the social worker.

But when he had tried to tell her why he *must* call Social Services, he sounded so broken that her nerve failed her. "Oh Wayne," she cried, "I'm so scared."

The little man poured the tea with trembling hands into two chipped cups with painted yellow roses.

"We prefer to get to know you as individuals," he said sadly, "before we get to know you as couples. Thank you for coming down by yourself on a working day."

Wayne felt a terrible compulsion to apologize. "I don't have to teach Friday afternoons anyway..." Maybe he wouldn't seem very dependable away from his post.

The social worker glanced at some forms.

"Of course," he murmured, "you teach at the university."

"I'm in the German department. Though I teach Icelandic, really."

160

It was the kind of obsessive qualification that could only make him look vacillating. Why couldn't he just shut up? But the fellow took out his pen and wrote "Icelandic" dutifully on the paper at his knees. The hand was as slender as an old woman's, one of the Norns.

"Would you like some more tea, Mr. Goodman?"

"Thank you," he replied with desperate concentration. Although the little ceremony offered   *here for Baldr*   a momentary security, ceremony itself would change too soon to interrogation.

The man hid one eye behind the raised teacup, looking him over.

"What we like to explore first in these sessions," he followed the predestined script, "is your background, parents, schooling, that sort of thing. We'd like to know as much as we can about your childhood."

"Where would you like me to start?"

"Why don't you start with your family? Tell me about your mother and father."

Wayne took a deep breath.

"I'm scared I'm more like my grandfather. But if I told you about him, you wouldn't dare give us a baby."

III
BALDR

Karen

Down the aisle behind us a baby fusses and fusses. What's wrong with the mother that she won't try to comfort it? You'd think she would know better than to drag an infant out on a night like this. What if the bus broke down and we had to wait in thirty below?

Mom sleeps like a baby herself, her huge face slumped close to my shoulder, crowding me into the window. The thought of actually sleeping in the same bed with her horrifies me. But what choice did I have as a child? I could only cling to the skirt of the mattress and try to keep from sliding down in the trough, burying my face in that back. We would lie that way, the one as stiff as the other, waiting for Connie to cry again. Once I asked why. Mom claimed it was for Dad's sake. But she knew it was a lie. She was looking out for her image of herself as a woman suffering for her family.

I stifle a laugh. It isn't hard; I only have to look at that cropped bullet-head in front of me. The old gent's a complete stranger. And yet he could pass for Mom's brother, two of a kind, the only kind that thrives in our heritage. I could tell he was Ukrainian the minute he got on at the Junction. The first thing he did was tilt his seat back as far as it would go. Without bothering to look back. When I stood up to ask him would he mind raising it a little, he stared at me like I was

165

crazy. *Oldstyle* Ukrainian, I thought, hating that obstinate face. The ogre in all of Mom's stories, her father refusing to hear a word of complaint from *Baba*. God knows she couldn't make the same complaint about Dad. But with Mom anything is possible. So if she's *newstyle* Ukrainian, what hope is there for me?

The way I feel, I might as well get off the bus right now at the mental home. But the tires pulsate in the seatback, telling my knees there aren't any more stops on these dark hills. The feeling of confinement is almost more than I can bear. I'm amazed Wayne couldn't hear it in my voice this morning.

"You're not going to believe this," his own voice sounded naked and amazed.

"We've won the lottery."

"Not quite the one you think. Mr Batchelar called. We're the parents of a baby boy."

"Oh my god."

My knees actually buckled. I sagged into the cheap leather recliner, just sitting and staring at the gloomy varnish of Mom's wainscotting.

"I said you wouldn't believe me."

"But how—" I groped for words "—when we're not due till June? I spoke to Mr Batchelar only last Friday."

"I know. He told me how sorry he was. But they can never be sure."

I didn't know what to say.

Wayne's voice was suddenly so soft, it brought tears to my eyes.

"It takes some getting used to, doesn't it? It caught me up short, too."

But I couldn't afford to be understood right then.

"That's it," I could hear my voice almost as hard as in the old days. "It's so sudden. What will you do? Cut short your trip?"

"There's no question of going any more. We have to be at Social Services at eleven in the morning to pick him up."

"Wayne, you know what you're going to be like if you don't find some answers."

He was silent. For an instant I saw Dad veiled in a cloud of cigarette smoke, bludgeoned into silence.

"I'm not so sure," Wayne sounded discouraged by more than just me, "there's anything in Trail for me to find out."

166

"But you know how depressed you're going to be if you don't make yourself into a novelist. Sometimes I think you'd rather be dead than—"

The receiver was as rigid as a hammer in my hand. Then I heard a catch in his breath.

"You may be right, Karen."

The way he spoke so very humbly, I knew that the trouble was me. I was falling behind again, I might never change.

"You know, it took me thirty minutes before I could make up my mind to call you? I've been so scared to be a father, Karen."

What did he think, that it was a Sunday School picnic? I could have told him a thing or two about scared.

"Would you like to hear what a big boy *he* is, at least?"

"Yes," I said numbly. I just couldn't imagine it.

"Over ten pounds," he sounded as proud as a natural father. As if he could have done the job himself.

"He's not a newborn," I feel I've got a right to be unreasonable. "They've mixed our file with someone else."

"I don't think so. The poor kid is really stuck with us, Karen. If the nurses will even give him up. Mr Batchelar says they dote on him, he's so cute."

Then I had just a flash of the poor girl, faceless but sad, her stitches still in her flesh while her baby was ripped from her a second time.

"I don't want it. Not yet, I mean. What if the birth mother decides to appeal before the thirty days? Shouldn't we wait till she has no legal claim on it?"

"Karen, for crying out loud, you're not—"

"Don't go jumping to conclusions. I didn't go through those interviews just because I'm a masochist, you know. But have you ever thought of the pain of surrendering a child when it finally had a face? Have you?" The line was dead. "Wayne?"

"No," I heard him talk my language, "I don't suppose it's the right thing to do if that's the way you feel. Do you want me to call Mr Batchelar and ask for foster care?"

Couldn't he see that bonding would take place, then, with some other woman? And I would never be the true mother?

"You know I hate to choose. It was my fault we didn't even pick a sex. You're just lucky it turned out to be a boy."

167

"You know that isn't true," he petted me. "You were the stronger one, more prepared to take whatever life gave you. Like the rest of the human race."

What a laugh!

He hesitated as if he read my mind, even over the telephone.

"It's natural to get cold feet, isn't it? We're only going through the stages natural parents do. Shall I make like a regular father and come out there and get you?"

It would take him away from his desk for the rest of the day.

"No," I answered too quickly, almost too vehemently. But I had to do something to make it appear I was choosing this baby, not just waiting to be carted off into motherhood. "Wayne, would it be alright if I brought Mom along to help?" I couldn't believe it, such folly I was speaking.

Suddenly I catch my dark reflection watching me from the glass of the bus window. The snowy fields race alongside, though farther out they stand empty to the horizon. Then I realize how deeply I've been kidding myself. All those ceramic classes up at Kelsey, do-it-yourself-automotive courses, you name it, I was only trying to prove I wasn't bare as Mother Hubbard's cupboard. Prove to whom? I certainly knew I wasn't creative like Wayne, I wasn't fooling myself that way. Maybe I only wanted to be sure he wouldn't find out in his novel who I really was. But I can't pretend to myself that I don't know why he chose me. I was sterile and I thought it made me free. So he could be free too, because my body relieved him of the necessity of reproducing himself.

Things used to be so simple before I was married. I was glad when my period didn't stop, because it got me away from home to the hospital. I couldn't mind the tubes stuck in my arm because they kept me from bleeding to death in little gushes.

"We can do a *curettage*," Dr Levitt said at last.

"Is it going to hurt?"

"You won't feel a thing," he said in his fatherly way, at least the way I imagined real fathers to be.

Mom didn't ask what it meant. In a way I was glad; I didn't want her to know about my body.

But Dr Levitt was right, it didn't hurt, not down there. The pain was all gathered in my head, chloroform hangover. And the nagging fear when the bleeding still hadn't stopped.

After several *curettages,* Dr Levitt admitted he was scared of cancer.

"I could do an operation guaranteed to prevent it," he said with his hands clasped over mine. "But then you couldn't have babies."

"I'm not going to have babies anyway," I said with a quick glance at Mom. I was surprised she looked so hurt. She always said not to bother coming home if I got pregnant. Out of wedlock was what she meant. But I assumed she must know we felt the same way about children. I wasn't going to let them ruin my life, or ruin theirs either, for that matter. Because how could I help myself from slashing at their legs with a broomstick like she did? Or drumming on their shoulders and arms with a cooking pot the minute I flew into a rage? I even hated to compete in field days because I was ashamed to be seen in shorts.

"Is there a chance," I looked away from Dr Levitt's kindly eyes, "that I could die from the operation?"

Dying itself, drugged out of existence, didn't faze me in the least. It was dying of cancer, slowly, in pain, that was too awful to consider.

"What do you think I am, some kind of a butcher?" Dr Levitt exaggerated his Jewish accent. Because he was Polish and understood Ukrainian, I always thought he was like us, but better.

"No," I laughed. But looking at Mom, I felt disappointed.

It wasn't until she had gone home, stopping first to brag to the nurse how brave I was to have my hysterectomy out, that I realized why. It had to do with something that had happened two years before. It was August, I remember, because the house was acrid with pickling vinegar that had boiled over on the stove. Mom wasn't home. She had taken off uptown as soon as Dad was back in the garage after lunch. I was left to feed my baby sister, but when Mom was gone so long, I got scared. We went around the east side of the house to be sure she hadn't come back to the garden without us noticing. The blades of corn rustled and clashed in the breeze. But the cucumber patch was deserted. Only a washtub full of cukes sat on the lawn. We were still there, kneeling in the grass to feel the prickly stems, when Mom came up the walk with a gallon jug of vinegar in her hand.

"Boże," she said panting a little, "that Mrs Sapach could talk all day. I told for her that I got to go home and do my pickles. So she told

the rest of the gossip she was saving." And cackled as if she'd really pulled one over on that Mrs Sapach.

I cackled too, proud to think that she could give me her confidence. While she took her jug to the house, I rooted with Connie in the tub for the thorniest cuke we could find. Connie shuddered with delight. Mom swore through the kitchen window. A plate crashed to pieces in the sink. The porch door slammed.

"What kind of daughter are you," she stopped short at sight of me, "that you can't help me nothing? I work all day so hard and you can't clean away your sister's plate!"

I sprang up from the tub, poised for flight.

"I'm sorry," I said in a rush. "Connie had to go to the bathroom and I forgot when we came back."

"When I was your age, I had five kids to look out for."

I didn't have to listen to the words, I knew it all by heart.

"Yeah, five kids," she recited her lie back to herself, since Auntie Phyllis was the eldest and did most of the child-raising. "And I scrubbed those wood floors every day soft as cloth. It wasn't even a house, just two rooms behind the poolroom with a curtain between. So how come you can't even look out for your little sister?"

"What do you think I was doing while you were out gossiping?"

"You don't talk smart for me."

"Mom!" I yelled in case the neighbours could hear. She only paused long enough to grab a cuke from the tub, then chased me like someone from the cartoons. Three times we circled the yard while Connie stood and wailed by the tub.

Mom stopped by the clothesline pole, leaning one hand on it, her chest heaving. She cleared her throat, hawking a bubble of phlegm into the grass.

"No wonder I'm so sick."

Suddenly it scared me to think of her fatty heart thudding away in that great, thick body.

"Maybe if you didn't get so mad—"

"You wait, you'll see," she glowered. "You'll find out when you're a mother. Being a mother makes you all the time so sick. My mother died...."

A shadow crossed her eyes, I saw how much she wanted to believe her life was almost the same. She ought to have been scared shitless that she'd end up like *Baba* in the mental hospital. But it wasn't the

170

asylum she ever remembered. It was only the T.B. Sanitarium with its coughing and spitting of blood.

Mom coughed and spat once more and I felt a stab of fear in my chest. How would I feel if she died after the way I had made her run? Her sudden lunge from the clothesline pole almost caught me short. But when I looked back, she had stopped, then was bending to pick up the heavy washtub.

"You'll have sometimes to come in the house," she said. "Don't think you can get away without paying nothing."

Connie toddled after her. After awhile I went uptown to Gloria Bordyko's house. Her father's shoe repair business was in the front of the house, on a level with the street. I went up the side of the grey-shingled building. The odour of leather filled the house as far back as the kitchen. But I liked it there; it smelled of masculine contentment and a quiet authority. Gloria could never understand why I wanted to stay inside when I went there to play. Once she even made me promise not to tell how she scrubbed with Sunlight soap to get rid of the smell of leather.

Gloria came out the screen door directly off the kitchen. I caught just a whiff of peace.

"Let's get the gang together in the hideout," she volunteered at once.

The hideout was just a nest among the willows along the creek, down past the elevators. It was a place where boys and girls could still be babes in the woods, scaring themselves with made-up horrors. But today I didn't feel much like playing good guys and bad guys. The afternoon dragged. When the gang trailed away for supper, I stayed on, feeling richly sorry for myself.

I only went home when the rustling in the bushes got too much for me. I sat on our high front step where I could be close to them in the light, hearing the phone ring and Mom gossiping as if nothing had happened. There was a slap of cards being shuffled, Dad playing solitaire in a cloud of grit and smoke. Even Connie didn't seem to miss me. She squealed and giggled, while Mom put her pyjamas on, the same way she did for me. The house sounded at peace, as if I was the only troublemaker.

A shadow fell across the square of light on the concrete. I shrank against the wall, hearing Mom clear her throat. But she didn't call out my name, or even ask Dad if he had seen me. I might have been dead for all she cared. But she knew I wasn't; she had left the door open. Then finally I understood why *Baba* was the only person she had ever loved. And I wished I was dead so my mother could love me too.

"Boy," Mom's voice startles me so that I bang my knee on the corner of the seat, "that little baby sure wants to cry!"

She sounds annoyed. It must have woke her up.

"You'd think the mother would be scared to venture out in weather like this," I say impartially.

"Hmmph," Mom snorts, "I don't blame her for wanting to step out. It gets so depressing to be all the time home and worry about your kids and your husband."

The old man in front sits up as if he's been kicked. I have to choke back a laugh. But at least I can stretch my knees out now, thanks to Mom.

"Sure," she goes on, "you remember at home how it was. The more I did good for Dad, the worse he used to get. I got so I didn't care no more. So never spoil your husband. As he is stronger than women, we're the weak ones."

I've seen how weak she is with Dad, alright. Like the time she caught him talking to Jeanette Rudachyk, the boarder in our basement. Mom kicked the bitch out the same day. But even when she finally listened to Dad—that he was only talking, Jeanette was someone who *liked* to listen—Mom went around telling the whole town that he couldn't get it up. I suppose it's his own fault for not leaving her long ago. Most likely he needed to pity himself.

"Not everyone is like you, Mom."

The wail of the baby stops short, as if the mother finally thought of sticking a bottle in its mouth. Then it spurts a protest, gagging on cold milk.

"I hope you get a good baby," Mom says with her usual timeliness and tact. "I hope it won't be all the time crying."

"Babies cry," I say as if it were something I dealt with every day.

"*Boże,*" she says in disgust, then I realize it's not with me. "I forgot to tell for you that Gloria Bordyko is pregnant. She said to pass a hi for you when they stepped in last week from Fort McMurray."

172

"I haven't seen her in years," I say guiltily, though I wouldn't care now to see her and her roughneck husband. When I needed to tell someone where the green and yellow bruises on my legs came from, I thought I could trust Gloria.

"She says she really wants to be a mother. Wait when it comes. She'll find out."

"That's all I've ever heard from you—what a woman has to suffer."

"Yeah," she doesn't even notice, "you'll find out like I did."

"Although I'm going to miss the birth pangs. Too bad, eh?"

"You're lucky, that's for sure. I didn't have nothing easy. I give up my happiness for my kids."

It's a broken record, no telling if she listens herself. How scared she used to be that I'd miss my share of misery, asking all the time, "Why don't you adopt a little baby?" It wasn't even my idea, just something I did for her. And Wayne.

Dear god, I can't have meant that. Not when it was me who pushed Wayne through the door of Social Services. Didn't he say we were happy the way we were? Mom only wants to be a *Baba* so she can hold her own with the other women. *Boże*, that would be the day I'd take so many pains for her sake. I must have felt empty because of my hollowed organs. And so I talked Wayne into it. Talked him as far as the door anyway.

It was those interviews I hated most. At least when you disrobed in a doctor's office, you still had flesh to cover you. But when you sat one on one in that tiny interview room, there was no hiding your nakedness of spirit. "How do you feel about spankings, Mrs Goodman?" the social worker asked the second or third time, hoping just once he'd get a right answer. "Would you spank your child?" At least I could tell the truth about that. "Isn't it necessary sometimes?" "I don't know." "Well, my Mom certainly whaled the daylights out of me." "Oh dear. Is that so. Tsk tsk. Statistics show that abused children turn into abusive parents."

At least there was some chance in the group interviews to hide in the herd opinion. But I was completely on my own again the day he asked us to write a personal essay. Wayne showed me his before he mailed it in. It was so measured, so deep and eloquent, that I despaired of writing anything like it. "The finest thing that's crossed my desk," Mr Batchelar said. "It's all there," he added as an afterthought, running his fingers through his fringe of sandy hair.

I tried not to let Wayne see I was lifting his ideas in my own words. But the main idea was something I never could fathom. "Children," he wrote, "give you your place among the generations." I wanted only to escape the generations by having someone else's baby.

"I know what you mean," I answer Mom the way she deserves. "Kids don't make you happy, that's for sure."

She beams at me as if we could be sisters.

"You're so lucky," she says wistfully. "I couldn't do nothing when my babies come. You can always send yours back if it's no good."

"Is that what you wanted to do with us?"

"We didn't have no money," she blusters. "I had to go with Dad to Windsor so he wouldn't have to go in the army. There was no one to keep Stevie when I had to work in that factory."

It's a long-playing broken record. And yet her grief is as fresh as on the day Auntie Phyllis boarded the train with Stevie, bound for Saskatchewan. I can't imagine having to give up my child like that. She wants to believe she lost him at that moment, the bond forever broken between mother and child. That that's the real reason he stays away in Ontario, now that he's a big lawyer.

"I'm sorry, Mom," I touch her briefly on the sleeve. But the way she stiffens shames me.

Then she nods as if she's a little unsure of herself. My heart beats like the wings of a trapped bird.

"Mom, do you remember that time Gloria Bordyko was sleeping overnight at our house and she put her own hair up in curlers?"

"Gloria was a good girl," Mom says. "She talked all the time so nice to me."

Gloria used to point at our stack of old Reader's Digests and ask, "What happened to your Dad's balls? Did your Mom quit using them for bookends?"

"Do you remember how you took me aside when Gloria went up the stairs to bed? And you said how smart Gloria was because she could do her own hair?"

"She was a good girl," Mom never gets the point. "She listened everything to what her Mother said."

"Do you remember, though, what else you said? Don't take it wrong, I just want you to know how it hurt. You said, 'I wish she was my daughter, not you.'"

174

"I didn't say no such thing!" her arm jerks back as from a blowtorch.

"Mom, it's alright now."

"Why do you always have to tell for me the bad things I did?" Faces are beginning to turn in the aisles. Mom looks to the old man in front for sympathy. I don't know where to look. "You really don't remember?" I say wanly. But memory only serves her when she's looking for revenge. Probably she thinks I'm just like her, nursing a grudge for the rest of my life. "I don't mean to hurt you, Mom. But isn't it time we understood one another?"

"You never quit like Gloria school in Grade nine," she says gruffly. "Why would I want her for a daughter?"

I sigh and look away out the window, watching the red beacons of the radio tower pass in the fields. The bus tops the last brief rise and there is Saskatoon like a spreading sea of light. My heart quickens at the sight. Saskatoon the Beautiful, City of Bridges. Words that once seemed like a bridge from my childhood to another life. But now I know there's no escape for me. I am going to make my child suffer because I'm just like my mother.

As we descend the railway overpass into Sutherland, the university shines like a city unto itself. My heart races over the dark fields of the experimental station. Wayne will be there to help me. He's saved me from being exactly like her—saved me by defending his own balls. Still I wish I didn't feel so stupid with him, as if I were always in the wrong.

It's his teaching has changed him. I ought to know better than anyone that it can be hazardous to your health. I used to get so depressed teaching Grade Ones that the only way I could help myself was to lash out at him. He took it because he knew I was scared to death of the responsibility. He told me later, when he started teaching at the University, that it was the same for him. He nearly shit himself every day the first couple of years. I don't know how he's managed to do it. Still his department has helped to spoil him. They gave him a reduced load to finish his novel. But being a writer is not the same thing at all as being an authority in his field. The more he tries to make his novel conform to his will, the more he ends defeated. His grandfather eludes him in story just as he did in life. He's said once or twice that he can't finish the book because he's

175

powerless to change a thing. We're both as helpless today as when we were children.

Both *were* helpless, at least, as late as this morning. Till the father took a child. The father took a child, hi-yo the merry-o—The bus grinds to a stop at a traffic light. I try to prop my knees against the seatback, but they are already wedged tight. So nothing has changed from our first years of marriage when we would both be braced for the reunion. My fault, then as now. But it's true that I would come back sounding as hard as Mom. Wayne used to say even my accent was changed, I sounded so Ukrainian. And I would ask him did he think he could lose me to my mother, of all people, in just two days? Then I would settle a pillow under my head, inviting nothing more than sleep. But when he took so long folding his trousers, I'd forget and snap, "Close the light." "I'm *shutting off* the light," he would say quietly, as if to emphasize just how far I'd gone away.

I don't resent it any more that he's refined the bohunk out of me. Yes, I do resent him. The way he was so damn proud on the phone this morning, as if he alone invented fatherhood. He's crazy if he's hoping this baby will let him rewrite the past. Because the past is the past, we're only angry spectators. Wayne has simply to look at Mom and me to see the truth of that.

I check to be sure she's not a mindreader. Her double chin is drawn up so tight, she seems as braced as I am. Against the meeting with Wayne? Or still against me?

"Mom," I touch her arm again. And lo, she suffers me. "I didn't mean to bring up that old stuff. I guess I've always been scared I wasn't a good enough daughter to you. That's all."

"You're a good daughter," she says shortly. "Not like Gloria Bordyko."

The bus gathers speed on the slope of the Twenty-Fifth Street bridge. Then I kick myself because I forgot to look for a light in the office beside the observatory. I don't know why I fret. Wayne will be there to meet me. The trees close overhead like the entrance to an igloo, so much hoar frost from open water on the river. High-rises glitter through the branches to our left. When we turn south into the warehouse district, I want to reach out and hold Mom's hand. But dignity prevents me; I must be the mother now.

As we pull into the bus bay, I pick out Wayne's moon face at once amidst the crowd inside the depot. He looks sober and intent, not at all as if his will had to be screwed up to meet me. His lips are always my sign. They are thick and wet, not drawn and white like they used to be. As he moves toward the door, I see he's wearing his brown cloth coat. He hasn't put on a scarf, or even done up his top button. I could crown him when I see his leather shoes slip on the icy pavement. I'm away for a weekend and he's as careless as he was the day we met in university.

Mom is out in the aisle reaching up for her coat. She hands me mine. *Carefree.* That's the word I wanted to describe his expression. How am I ever going to put on a face to meet him now?

Mom lets me go down the aisle in front of her.

"Hi," Wayne smiles a shy, crooked little smile I haven't seen in years. Then his smile widens to include Mom as well. "Hello *Baba*," he stumbles a little on the formality. But I can see he's holding nothing back.

"*Boże*," Mom plunges right in, "it's a good thing for your baby you were still home."

"It's a good thing for the baby," he purses his lips ironically, "that I didn't light out for the territories."

My laughter is too giddy. The bus driver gives me a funny look, reaching another suitcase out of the belly of the bus. But Wayne doesn't notice.

"I told the social worker my wife was out of town and I hated to have a baby without her."

"You idiot," I slip my hand through his arm.

"Give for me that box," Mom grabs at the string before the driver slams it on the pavement. She's brought food, as usual, to pay her own way. I should be grateful. But her *pyrohy* is all I find edible any more. Wayne has taught me to enjoy good food, among other things.

Still I don't look at him when we near the car.

"Here, Mom, you climb in the front with Wayne."

Once you get old, you shouldn't have to wrestle with a two-door coupe. But when I steal a look at him, he doesn't seem to mind. So why should I be disappointed?

"So, Marcella," he says getting in, "are you ready to be a grandmother?"

177

I brace myself, not sure which side to be on. But he really means it, he's not being ironic. He even called her Marcella! Hell, he's never acted before as if she had a name.

"*Boże,*" Mom doesn't seem at all surprised, "I'm just glad to get away from my home. I haven't been going no place as it's so cold. Dad never wants to go no place anyways."

"I suppose it gets lonely for you," Wayne says generously. "Well, you'll have your hands full helping Karen these next few days. I'm glad you could come."

I look at his snub nose in profile, at his hair cut straight as a shingle above his ear, and wonder how anything so familiar could feel so strange. But I see what I missed at first meeting. He's free, not simply carefree.

When we stop at last in the alley behind the house, it's as if I am having to translate the word *home*. My dream house come true. Wayne and I used to park in front of it and neck, gloating over the lights of the city, greedy for one another. "One day when you're a professor," I used to joke, "that's the house we're going to live in." I didn't believe him the day he came home to say the widow had died, he'd just got a call from the realtor. Saskatchewan Crescent was too expensive, we couldn't afford it. But Wayne proved with pencil and paper that we could manage.

"I need to talk to Wayne," I warn Mom when we leave him to put the car in the garage. "I hope you don't mind. We'll go straight upstairs to bed."

"*Boże,*" she doesn't seem to notice, "I sure wish Dad had bought for me a house like this."

It is they who have taken sides against me, both in cahoots.

Wayne comes struggling up to our bedroom with both suitcases just as I am slipping out of my bra.

"*Boże,*" he says with averted eyes, making me feel worse, "you sure ran away from her in a hurry."

"You go talk to her," my resentment gets away on me. "If you're such bosom buddies."

The bacon fat tinges a cloudy grey before it puckers and begins to run out of itself. Then it turns rosy and I flip each strip as quickly as I can with shaky hands. Wayne likes his bacon soft, and I've learned to prefer it that way too. Mom used to fry it stiff as boards, then leave it to soak in a pool of grease. She'd be in here now, ruining breakfast. But *The Price is Right* is on TV.

"Are you going to let that thing blare all day once the baby comes?" I say from the door to the dining room.

"Looo-k," she points like a child, "that lady guessed two hunderd forty nine dollars and she won for her husband such a nice boat."

"I'm surprised," I won't give up the point, "you're not watching *Family Feud.*"

"I don't like him no more, that *Hogan's Heroes* guy. He kisses all the time so many women."

Maybe Wayne would see I'm on his side if I made him go to Trail. He mustn't lose his grandfather's story now because of me. Not when he was so very nearly free of the hurt of his own past.

Damn, now I've fried the shit out of the bacon. Mom should feel right at home. I only have to soak it in its grease.

"Good morning," Wayne says at the nape of my neck. I jump halfway out of my mules. Then, without looking at his face, I glide into his arms like an underwater swimmer.

"Oh Wayne," I wail, "I feel like such a shit."

His arms are my rope net; but his voice is hollow, more depressed than I feared.

"You're not the only one. Who are we trying to kid?"

"You've been so brave," I blubber. "I'm the one who's dragging you down."

I can feel something like breakage from his chest, the sound of crashing china, anthem of my youth. Then in amazement I hear him crying with me, not ashamed to seem weak. Slender as the willow he weeps, bending before he breaks.

"Darling," I say over and over, rocking with him, "sweetheart, I'm so sorry."

In time he recovers himself enough to try to tell me. But his voice, usually so sure, is small and uncertain.

"The day Charlie died—" his breath convulses, choking off the words.

"I know," I say soothingly, "I know what you feel."

"I'm not so sure," his pride makes him speak more certainly. "The day my little brother lay there in that pool of blood and dirt, all I could think of was that my granddad had to pay. Karen, I'm scared. I guess I've been scared all my life of having a child I could lose."

The doctor's eyes are filling with sweat. Through his mask I see him gulping fresh air. Then he ducks back under the tent drawn over my knees. I feel something begin to give, now burst in a hot fountain of blood. Then my life is sweeping out on that tide

"We won't lose him," I burrow against him. "You're going to fly out there today and break the old troll's spell. Didn't you say once that no father, not even him, could leave just a death wish to his kids?"

"It's been two years already. What am I going to find that Mom and Dad missed?" He draws his face back from my hair. "What if there's really nothing there, Karen?"

"You've got to go find out for your son's sake."

He is hushed, mustering every ounce of resolve.

"I'd probably be looking in the wrong place. It would be so damn easy to blame him for all my failings."

"Sure it would. And the next thing you know, I couldn't blame my mother either."

He bears my scorn quietly. "Would that be such a bad thing?"

I can't answer. I hide in his arms, pressing against him. But the silly jackass gets a hard on!

"Wayne, let go. I don't want Mom to see us like this."

I have to push him away, knowing I have no place left to hide.

"You know," I say with my face toward the refrigerator, "what I'm like around her."

"It doesn't matter," he says without conviction.

"Why don't you go call the airline and see if you can still get on? And leave me to finish burning breakfast?"

A strangled chuckle escapes him, breaking the ice.

"If I do go out there, I'm not coming back till I've discovered his secret with women."

The diningroom door flaps. I might as well go whole hog and pretend to the world that he can't get it up. *Boże*, why do I have to do everything in my power to be like Mom?

I fish the bacon out of the fat and set it on a paper towel to dry. Our honeymoon was over the first night we came home, stepping in at Mom and Dad's. I don't know why I didn't see it coming, the way I had lashed out the day before in Minot at some crude joke Wayne made. A wedding car had zoomed by us with old shoes and tin cans writhing beneath the bumper. "Everybody knows what they'll be doing tonight," said my knight in shining armour. But I was scandalized, I see at last, because everybody *did* know, and I couldn't lie to Mom any more.

The swinging door flaps and Wayne is back in the room.

"I'm confirmed," he says, leaning up against the cupboard. "But are you really sure you want me to take off this soon? I'd have to get you to whisk me straight to the airport. And you'd have to drive the baby home alone."

"What do you think I am, incompetent?" I answer rashly.

"Alright, let me put it this way. Think of all the time you're going to have alone with him. You'll get to know him before I do. Do you think that's fair?"

"It's only natural," I try to joke. Then I can finally let go in the shelter of his strength. "Oh Wayne, I'm scared. I'm just so scared of bringing up a child the way I am."

"There's nothing wrong with you," his hand strokes my head, "that your maternal instincts won't cure."

But I know all about instinct. Instinct is the thing that keeps me from changing.

"The French toast is burning."

"Damn!" Now I can't even cook. Mom was right, he is too good for me. I should have had a man who beats me. Then I wouldn't feel so bad.

"Pour the coffee," I bitch in spite of myself. "I can't do everything alone."

In the other room I hear him say, "Breakfast is served," as if he made it himself.

At the table I notice how Mom's bulging face has turned almost childlike. "It's such a lucky thing for the baby you weren't gone yesterday," she repeats last night's formula. Her cheeks aren't so puffed, even her mastoids look less sunken. For a moment I feel as if she really did look this way when we were born...she wasn't just keeping up with the Jonuks.

"Yeah, it's a good thing I didn't light out for Trail right away," Wayne says easily. They are both into re-runs. "I waited till today at least to run away."

"You could still go if you wanted." As usual, Mom hasn't bothered to listen. "You don't need to worry a thing. Two women should take care of one little baby."

"It's kind of you to offer. I'm not sure I'll go," he looks at me. Her reply takes no notice of his courtesy.

"All the ladies in Nisooskan want to stay in their homes, not to be travelling with their husbands. You know Mrs. Annie Ginetz, how her husband is all the time going places to his brother in Vancouver and he wants her to be with him? She says, 'I wouldn't go no place with him. I'll show for him.' And you know she bought herself a little car? Yeah. She drives around town all the time and to so many farms to be with the ladies. The women around Nisooskan, they don't want to be with their husbands, that's for sure."

"What makes you think I'm like you?" I thump the table till the dishes rattle. "What makes you think I don't want to go everywhere with my husband? Can't you do anything besides bitch about men all the time? Jesus, I'm so sick of your bloody bitching. I'm sick of the sound of—" *Your voice,* I realize at last, isn't the only thing I want to run away from.

"Karen," Wayne calls after me. Then I hear him say excuse me as I rush out through the kitchen.

"Karen, wait," he catches at the bathroom door before I can shut it completely. Oh, I am even worse now than she is.

"Hey," he says softly, "you were superb. I didn't know you did impersonations."

I can't hold the door any longer. But neither can I laugh at these tears. I have no choice except to bawl like the poor kid who's going to have to put up with me.

"Oh Wayne, didn't you see her face when I hit the table? She looked—almost afraid of me. What will I become when my own mother is afraid of me?"

"It's a problem, alright," he says with a funny little laugh. Then I feel the bob of his Adam's apple against my crown. "Karen, you've got every right to be mad. At me as much as her."

I look up so swiftly that he stiffens.

"What do you mean?"

"I'm scared of your anger, I guess. I wouldn't put it past me to want a martyr like my mother."

I hold his eye, feeling as if we've set foot at last on even ground.

"There you go yourself, trying to take the blame for the way I am. It's me who should get out there and apologize for all my fuss."

I reach behind his back for some toilet paper to dab at my eyes.

"What do you want to do? Scare her to death?"

My face cracks, a film of ice I didn't know was there. And then I am laughing—softly for Mom's sake—but truly laughing, perhaps for the first time in years. In the mirror over Wayne's shoulder I catch sight of running mascara, a face too hollow to be thought pretty any more. But I guess I can stand it if he can.

"Karen, I don't need to go to Trail. My grandad's not there. He's waiting in the book I have to finish. He's sure to see me get my share of pain. But maybe we can see to it that our son gets none."

Hope sends my voice high and seeking.

"Wayne, are we going to make all the same old mistakes with our son? Or do you think it will help because we're not his maker?"

He looks at me as if he'd like to soften the blow.

"Who ever learned a thing from being told? He'll have to go through it all again, same as us." And smiles that crooked smile he wore for my homecoming last night.

"Hey, you'd better get a leg on, girl. You don't want to be late when you're having a baby."

I look at my watch. 10:19.

"Boże, I've still got to pack a diaper bag!"

"Do you want me to clean up the breakfast things?"

"You could help me more, I think, by telling Mom why we've got to rush out of here. Then could you warm up the car?"

"At your service, Madame," he courts me out of the bathroom.

I fly up the thickly-carpeted stairs without daring to look at the river or the city beyond. The navy bag is in the closet in his room. Why didn't I leave myself more time? It's like making the usual dash to the hospital.

I try to decide between a blue sleeper and a yellow one with a bear cub on the front. I choose the bear cub as the better sign of his identity. I turn to grab a little undershirt from the top drawer of his chest, and then the powder from on top. What else? Diapers. My god, I nearly forgot the most important thing. Three Pampers should tide us over. I take four to be sure. The formula is supposed to come with him from the hospital, I know.

I hurry down the stairs with bag in hand, though now it is as if the bag hurries me, I'm not really in command of myself. Mom stands in the vestibule, clenching and unclenching her fists. She doesn't see me yet. She looks so oddly helpless in her great-fisted fidgeting, quite as harassed as I am.

"I put for you your coat in the living room," she says in her agitation.

"Thanks." I take my boots out of the closet where the coat usually hangs. "I shouldn't have snapped at you at the table," I say awkwardly.

She finds it as difficult to take an apology as I do to give it.

"I hope the baby doesn't cry for you," she says ritually.

"Babies cry. I'm not hoping for miracles." I needn't press her further.

"Good luck," she gives the first blessing I have ever had from her. There is no hug or anything like that. Her word of wellwishing is enough.

"Thanks. When I see you next, I guess I'll be a mother."

"Good luck," she repeats herself nervously.

Then I am hurried out the door and down the snowy steps. There are no tracks before me. Wayne must have gone out through the kitchen. I am aware, when I turn up the back walk, of Mom's neckless head thrust out the door. I wave once, then put out a hand to steady myself against the high stucco wall. I mustn't let my feet get away on me. Wayne is usually so good about waiting.

The cold swathes my head like a crisp new bandage, before the hurt begins to sting. I think of that summer night when Wayne came home from playing tennis. He had slipped on gravel and fallen, with all his weight, on one finger. The nail was torn off, meat split to the bone, right up to the knuckle. Blood surged out of the gash and splashed onto the sidewalk.

"For god's sake," I said, "do you have to go at tennis like it was fencing or something?"

I couldn't look at the hand, couldn't even watch while he washed it and disinfected and dressed it himself. I sulked out in the gazebo all the time he was tending to himself. I knew in my bones he should be getting stitches. The ragged way it healed proved me right. But I couldn't bring myself to look at the open flesh. To take responsibility for it. As if I couldn't forgive myself for being human.

I blunder through the cloud of fog billowing out the garage door, then grope till my mittened hand catches the handle of the car door.

"Have you got the baby's seat up from the basement?" I ask before I see it in the back. "Not that I think we'll need it."

Our silver Monte Carlo backs through its own grey exhaust. Then mercifully I can see again: the snowrutted lane, garbage cans, backs of houses...all so terribly confining. The car leaps ahead. Something high in my tummy leaps with it. I make no sound. Wayne is hushed and determined over the wheel, thinking his own thoughts.

We come out at the top of the Broadway bridge, before the traffic gets away at Five Corners. Steam from the river hangs beneath us, though down by the repeating arches of the Twenty-fifth Street bridge I see ice bunching near the shore...such an icy feeling here in the pit of my stomach.

The bridge tilts downtown. We slide helplessly on the ice for a moment. The car skids and straightens, Wayne has veered onto Fourth Avenue to avoid the red light on Nineteenth Street. There are so many things I still need. I wish we could stop for a moment at the Army and Navy. The parking mall is packed with cars for the January White Sale. Mom and I can go down tomorrow. No, tomorrow is Wednesday closing.

My thoughts race to First Avenue. There is the building on the left, standing in the shadow of the Centennial Auditorium. Wayne stops the car right in front of the door. The parking meter is vacant, just what the doctor ordered. Wayne comes round and takes my arm, drawing me out forcibly. Why am I so nervous? I'm as bad as Mom was before we left the house.

My heart pounds as we enter the flat, squat building. There are no windows. I feel suffocated.

The nurse takes my arm and helps me into the tiny room. There isn't much time, there isn't even time to stop it. They strap me onto the castor bed, fitting my feet to the cold metal stirrups. My ankle is clamped so I can't budge. And now we are rolling so quickly, the acoustic tiles on the ceiling flit by like swallows. I don't think we're going to make it. I give a final, brief whimper.

185

"Are you alright?" Wayne squeezes my hand so tightly. We are seated in a small airless room. Three plastic chairs are grouped at one end, a baby's crib at the other. "You look so white, Karen. Are you sure you want to go through with it? Am I forcing my choice on you?"

I choke back my tears. My husband knows this terrible thing about me, has known and always accepted what I couldn't accept about myself. I never wanted to give birth. I was relieved to be spared that fierce pain; I could never stand the thought of that much blood. He knew it before he married me. And still he put up with my only hope of having a family. I feel a fount of love for him well up in my belly, filling my barrenness.

"I'm sure," I let my eyes fill in the blanks, "it's the only way for someone like me. Hold my hand, love. Please hold onto me."

Then the door opens. Mr Batchelar stands there like a bashful child, looking so thin and woebegone in his wrinkled brown suit. The nurse appears, cradling a sleeping bundle.

"Who wants to hold him?" she says softly, lovingly.

Wayne stands up, my hands must have told him my knees won't hold me. She lifts the rounded blue blanket into his arms.

"There," she says reverently, "isn't he a little darling?"

I cling lightly to Wayne's elbow, getting to my feet.

"Look," he says, "look at what fat cheeks he's got. Precious little pup."

My heart balloons at the sight of those bulging cheeks, the tiny clenched fists. But his tightly shut eyes are so black and blue!

"What's wrong with his eyes?" my voice falters.

"Just bruises from his passage in the birth canal," Mr Batchelar says reassuringly. "He's had quite a hard trip of it, all told."

We stand another moment, adoring the miracle of his presence.

"Do you want to hold him?" Wayne asks so tenderly.

"Yes," my heart swells and enfolds him already, "yes. Oh yes, please."

186